Sexy Beast

a novel by Andrew Donkin
from the screenplay by
Louis Mellis and David Scinto

Sexy Beast

FILMFOUR 4

First published 2000 by FilmFour Books
an imprint of Macmillan Publishers Ltd
25 Eccleston Place, London SW1W 9NF
Basingstoke and Oxford

www.macmillan.co.uk

Associated companies throughout the world

ISBN 0 7522 7179 2

A CIP catalogue record for this book is available from
the British Library.

Typeset by SX Composing DTP, Rayleigh, Essex
Printed in Great Britain by Mackays of Chatham plc, Chatham, Kent

Based on the Recorded Picture Company and FilmFour film *Sexy Beast*, written by
Louis Mellis and David Scinto, produced by Jeremy Thomas
and directed by Joanthan Glazer. © 2000 Sexy RPC Ltd, Kanzaman S.A. and FilmFour Ltd.

Contents

1. Let's rock

The sun blazed in the sky like a ball of pure hate. Around it, a perfect deep blue firmament stretched away to the horizon in every direction. There were no clouds or birds to interrupt the view, nor any aeroplanes to break the glorious sun-baked silence.

Sprawled out on a sunbed, Gal Dove was slowly but surely being roasted alive. The hot-water bottle of spare, baggy flesh around his waist was turning a brighter shade of lobster red with every passing hour.

'Not like fucking England. Hot! Hot! Hot!' Gal muttered to himself. 'This is fucking hot.'

Gal struggled to slide himself further down the length of the sun-lounger, trying to find a more comfortable position in which to reach critical burn. His powerful but now gone-to-seed body was already deeply tanned. Not a two-week holiday tan or even the bronzing from a long heatwave summer. Gal's skin had the wonderful burnt and baked-in leathering of someone who lives in the sun all year.

The surface glistened with a clear, silver sheen, every inch heavily oiled with – as the bottle's tacky label screamed – 'Hawaiian Tropic Suntan Lotion'. The pungent scent of pineapples and coconut milk filled Gal's nostrils whenever he inhaled.

Hawaii-Five-O? Jack Lord, eat your fucking heart out.

Gal picked up a bottle of San Miguel from the table next to him and thirstily drained the last few drops. He gently put the empty bottle down by his side with the half a dozen others that had been his afternoon's work, then leaned back in his chair again.

'Look at this. This is fucking glorious. What a super fucking day. Superb weather. Fucking sun. Lovely, brilliant, tasty, fucking sun!'

Protecting his eyes were a pair of stylish black sunglasses, bought for Gal by his lovely wife, Deedee. On each hand, his fingers were covered by thick gold rings, bought for Gal by his lovely wife, Deedee. Nestling in the hair of his chest – just above the rising ripples of stomach flab – was a heavy gold chain, bought for Gal by his lovely wife, Deedee.

At the end of the patio to Gal's right was the large, white-painted house where Gal shared his slow and hot and wonderful life with Deedee. At the other end of the patio was a large swimming pool full of cooling, crystal-clear water. Deep under the water, the tiles at the bottom of the pool were in the design of two giant blue hearts – one touching the other. So fucking romantic.

Beads of fresh sweat burst out all over Gal's pink forehead. He felt them running races down the side of his brow and sighed with satisfaction.

'Oh, yeah. Bloody hell. I'm sweating like a porker here. I'm roasting. Baking. Boiling. It's like a fucking furnace, that sun. You could fry an egg on my stomach. You could fry a slice of fucking bread. Who wouldn't lap this up?'

Behind Gal, a small figure was listening to his whispered weather report. Enrique, wandering around the patio half-heartedly clutching a broom, could never understand why his English boss was so obsessed by something as simple as the sun.

'It's ridiculous!' continued Gal, getting louder. 'Tremendous! It's just fantastic! It's fan-dabby-dozy-tastic!'

Gal mopped the sweat from his forehead and suddenly became aware of Enrique's presence nearby. Or, more particularly, Gal became aware of Enrique's inactivity. The fourteen-year-old was sweeping the patio with such a minimum of effort that it was hardly noticeable that he was doing it at all. His skinny brown legs, sticking out from his shorts, were almost like broom handles themselves.

Gal leaned round and cleared his throat.

'Come on! Give it some!' he shouted. 'I don't pay your bloody wages to watch you stand still.'

'Zis brushes iz sheet!' said Enrique defensively.

'What?'

'Iz sheet!' he repeated, waving the brush at Gal.

'That's a good brush. There's nothing wrong with that,' countered Gal. 'What's the matter with ya? Don't blame the bloody brush – it's the man that counts. It's down to you and your technique. You're flipping lazy, ain't ya? The brush indeed, I don't know.'

Enrique took a firmer grip of the brush and resumed sweeping, this time with considerably more effort. Gal watched him, satisfied with the boy's newly-found energy.

'That's it! Get on with it!'

Enrique turned his back on his employer.

'Oh, now he's in a huff. Now he's sulking. You sulking, boy? Got the strop?' bellowed Gal. 'You wanna grow up,

3

mate, you do!' Then he lay back on his sunbed and once more turned his face towards the sky.

Gal took a deep breath, and his huge chest rose then fell as he exhaled slowly.

'I'm fucking dying here. This is fucking doing me in.'

Gal's fingers reached out and felt blindly for the table next to him. They found it and wandered spider-like towards a clear glass bowl containing iced water and a small white flannel. Gal lifted the flannel, squeezing out the excess water.

He sneaked a quick glance over the black rims of his sunglasses to make sure that Enrique wasn't watching, then carefully folded the flannel into a rectangle and laid it on his crotch.

The relief was instant.

Behind Gal, Enrique continued to grudgingly half-sweep the patio. His long dark mane of hair whipped back and forth as he moved. He muttered something derogatory under his breath, making sure it was incomprehensible but just loud enough for Gal to hear.

'What's that? You slagging me off? I bet you are, you little bugger,' responded Gal without looking round. 'You must think I'm a right fucking mug! You turn up here and get paid for doing nothing. I don't know how you get away with it! Put your back into it – mush!'

Enrique gave the patio two or three very enthusiastic sweeps with the broom and then lost all pretence of interest. He picked up a yellow swimming flipper that had been discarded by the edge of the pool. It was several sizes too big for him, but he pressed his foot inside anyway.

'Bloody lazy,' continued Gal. 'It's not like England here. Fucking Spain, it's a dump. Who am I kidding? Don't make me laugh. Grey, grimy England. Sooty stinking little

4

shit-hole. What a toilet! Every cunt walking around all day with a long face. Shuffling about, moaning and worried. No bloody thanks, not for me! People say, "Do you miss it, Gal?" I say, "No bloody way."'

Enrique jumped into Gal's field of vision, dancing joyfully around the patio, slapping the giant yellow flipper hard against the concrete. Gal was too busy with his rant to register this little display.

'They say, "What's it like in Spain then?" And I say, "It's hot, hot, hot. Fucking hot." "Too hot?" they say. "Not for bloody me," I tell 'em, "because I love it!"'

Enrique's flipper-leaping had taken him all around the pool and was now leading him back, one slap at a time, towards Gal.

'It is hot though, cor. Bloody hell.'

Enrique spiralled around to face Gal with a grin – and Gal finally noticed him again.

'Oi! I'm not paying you to flap about. Go into the kitchen and get us a couple of beers, will ya!' he ordered.

Enrique didn't need to be asked twice. He kicked off the flipper, sending it high into the air, then sprinted towards the house.

'Not that you bloody deserve one!' Gal yelled after him.

With considerable effort, Gal swung his legs over the edge of the sunbed and stood up.

'This heat is bloody killing me,' he announced, stretching his arms wide and opening his mouth in a great elephant yawn.

A movement in the distance caught Gal's eye. To the west, a small blue bay cut sharply into the rolling hillside. A fishing boat was bobbing through the water, casting out a line of ripples in its path.

Gal could see two local fishermen standing on the ship's deck, arguing – probably about which of them was going to clean the nets when they were back on shore. Behind the two quarrelling men, the wooden deck of the old boat was covered with their afternoon's harvest pulled from the warm sea.

In the house, Enrique was now in the cool kitchen, standing by the open door of the biggest of Gal's four fridges. He was hurriedly eating his way through a chilled chocolate bar, pilfered from inside the fridge. He gulped down the final piece, grabbed two bottles of beer, and then slammed the door shut with the palm of his hand. He ran out to where Gal was waiting by the pool.

'Beer!'

Gal studied the smile that played around Enrique's mouth.

'Is that chocolate?' he asked, pointing at the boy's chin.

'Iz no.'

Enrique sheepishly wiped his mouth with the back of his hand. There was nothing there. Gal smiled at his own cleverness.

'Bleedin' gotcha, didn't I?'

Gal rewarded himself with a long swig of cold beer.

'Soon we go hunting again with Mr Aitch, yes?' asked Enrique, eager to change the subject. 'This time I bring my father's gun.'

Enrique moved his arms as if aiming an imaginary gun at the barren hillside beyond Gal's patio.

'You can bring the gun, as long as you don't bleedin' shoot us, all right?' agreed Gal.

Enrique nodded, took a swig of his own beer and pulled a disgusted face.

Far up on the rocky hillside behind Gal, something started to move. A large round boulder about five feet in diameter tipped slowly over, its battered, rough bulk crushing the bush in front of it. As it began rolling directly towards Gal's patio and Gal himself, it began to pick up speed.

Gal would never discover what mysterious force had first disturbed the one-ton rock and set it in motion. Perhaps the extreme heat of the sun had caused part of the hill to crack and subside. Maybe rabbits, burrowing into the earth around the rock, had dislodged it. Or maybe other children from the nearby village had grown so jealous of Enrique's employment that they had decided to vent their feelings and levered the boulder free. The most likely explanation, though, was that God had simply decided to let Gal know that he was still paying attention.

Whatever the instigation, the killer boulder was now careering down the hillside.

On his patio, Gal bent down to pick up a small hand-held fan. He switched it on and was blessed with instant relief when the tiny, white plastic blades flicked into life. They buzzed around the central column like a swarm of obedient flies in orbit.

'That's better. That's lovely,' said Gal, fanning his cooked face.

He was completely oblivious to the boulder, now only yards away. It smashed down the hill, crushing everything in its path, speeding straight towards Gal.

2. Deep impact

Several miles along the valley from Gal's house, a sleek white sports car was racing along the road. Its fast-spinning wheels churned up a thick cloud of dust in its wake.

'That top'll look fantastic on you,' said Deedee, turning the steering wheel hard as the car sped around a steep curve.

'It's going straight back if it doesn't,' replied Jackie, flicking long blonde strands of hair out of her face.

The back of the car looked like a clothes shop on wheels. It was a fifty-minute drive to the city, and the girls were on the return journey from one of their regular shopping trips. One of their regular take-no-prisoners, husband's-credit-card-account shopping trips. Haphazardly strewn across the car's rear seats was a collection of designer packages and expensive-looking carrier bags advertising names like Chanel and Gucci.

'I'm gonna save the yellow undies for the weekend,' announced Jackie, nodding at her decision. 'Gotta keep Aitch interested, haven't I?'

'I don't think you've got any problems there. Just be careful you don't give him a heart attack – that's your only worry,' grinned Deedee conspiratorially.

'Here we are,' said Jackie, pointing to a barely noticeable dirt turning leading off from the main road.

'I love driving out here,' said Deedee, throwing the car into a tight turn that threw up even more dust.

A short way down the drive was the villa that Jackie shared with Aitch. As the car pulled up, the front door opened. A small white poodle called Noodle darted towards the car, yapping a greeting. Behind the dog, at a slower pace, followed the tall, skinny figure of Aitch, wearing white shorts and shirt, and deck shoes. A good twenty-five years older than Jackie, Aitch's silver hair and world-weary expression did nothing to hide his advancing years.

He smiled as he watched Jackie angle her long tanned legs to ease herself out of Deedee's car.

'Ooh, here they are – the pillagers return home! You been spending my money? Is that me skint again?' grinned Aitch.

'I made sure she went easy this time,' offered Deedee, smiling in return.

'Yeah, but your idea of easy and mine ain't necessarily the same thing, are they?' said Aitch, expanding his grin to show off his large, white teeth.

Jackie busied herself collecting her packages from the back seat, while Noodle insisted on jumping up at her, demanding attention.

'Is this me or you?' asked Jackie, holding a small package wrapped in a single red ribbon towards Deedee.

'You, I think,' said Deedee.

Jackie picked four more bags from the rear seat, then was too laden to manage any more. She looking meaningfully at Aitch.

'Bloody hell, Jack, you shoulda just towed the shop back,' he commented indulgently. 'Deedee, you're becoming a bad influence on my girl. We're gonna have to have a very serious talk about this, Jacqueline. I'm getting very worried about this shopping addiction you've got. It's spiralling out of control.'

'It's not shopping, these days it's called retail therapy,' offered Deedee, with a grin.

'I'm the one that'll need bleeding therapy by the time you two have finished with me,' said Aitch, surveying Jackie's shopping bounty. 'Did you get anything for me?'

'Yeah, a gag,' retorted Jackie. 'Now shut up and make yourself useful. Take some of these inside and then put the kettle on.'

'Yes, memsahib!'

Aitch shuffled forward, doing his best to look like a down-trodden slave, and scooped the bags from out of Jackie's hands. Then he shuffled towards the house, hampered both by the number of packages he was carrying and by Noodle, who was bouncing around his ankles.

'Noodle, just for once, will you get out from under my feet?' demanded Aitch. He paused in the doorway and looked back to Deedee, still sitting in the driver's seat. 'You stopping for a brew?'

'Thanks, Aitch, but I'd better get back. Gal will start wondering where I am. We'll see you later, yeah?'

'Are we coming to you, or are you coming here?' asked Aitch.

'You're coming to us. Gal's planning another barbecue.'

'I'll bring a fire extinguisher,' said Aitch. 'What sorta time?'

'Oh, get in that house, you! Mush!' ordered Jackie, cutting him short and waving Deedee goodbye.

Deedee put the car into gear, turned it around quickly,

and then sped away, churning up stones in the dirt track as she accelerated.

At that exact second, Gal, cooling his face with the hand-held fan, took two steps forward. That small movement saved his life. The huge boulder smashed through the patio wall and hurtled past the spot where Gal had been standing a moment before.

The rock flattened his sunbed, rolling over it and transforming it instantly into piece of twisted and broken scrap metal. In the next second, the boulder crashed into the swimming pool, throwing up a huge wave of water with its impact. Gal stopped dead as a wall of relatively cold water crashed into him from the side, almost knocking him off his feet.

'Jesus Christ!'

Enrique, taking empty beer bottles back to the kitchen, froze in shock.

Gal, now utterly drenched, blinked in stunned surprise, trying to clear his eyes of pool water. His once proud hair was soaked into a flat, institutional fringe.

Almost dazed, Gal stumbled towards the edge of his pool as Enrique came to join him. Together they stared down into its clear water where the huge rock had now settled.

'Fucking hell,' said Gal, slowly. 'Fucking ... fucking ... fucking ... hell.'

'It came from there,' said Enrique unnecessarily, pointing to the hillside beyond Gal's crushed patio wall.

'I know where it fucking came from. It nearly killed me. Did you see that? That overgrown pebble nearly fucking had me. Jesus – look what it's done to my bloody pool.'

Gal got down on his hands and knees and began peering through the water at the boulder.

'Come on,' he ordered, slipping into the water. Enrique followed suit and they both pushed themselves below the surface and swam towards the rock.

Gal's hands made contact with its rough surface. He felt his feet touch down on the bottom of the pool and pushed up against the bulk of the rock. He quickly realized that it was an impossible task. The boulder was stubbornly lodged in place and all Gal was doing was cutting his palms open. Suddenly running out of breath, he and Enrique pushed off to the surface simultaneously.

'Bloody hell. Do you see the size of that fucker? This is the bleeding asteroid that killed the dinosaurs,' gasped Gal, receiving only an expression of puzzlement from Enrique.

Gal gulped in another large lungful of air and dived down once more. He reached the boulder and pushed himself downwards to examine the bottom of the pool. The fucking thing had settled bang in the middle of the melting hearts design, effectively breaking it in two. Looking closely, he watched the current carry some small bits of dirt down into the cracks it had made in the tiles. Damn. The damage went right the way through – his pool was leaking.

Gal gestured to Enrique to help him try and move the rock one more time.

In the driveway, a white sports car was coming to a slightly too abrupt halt. Deedee turned off the ignition and got out. Unusually, Gal was nowhere to be seen.

'Gal?'

Deedee gathered her collection of packages and headed for the house. She was nearly at the kitchen door before she spotted the unfamiliar dark shape in the centre of the swimming pool.

What the fuck was that?

Gal had once earned his living through illegal activities underwater, but even he couldn't hold his breath for ever. His efforts to shift the enormous boulder were growing ever more hopeless when he peered up through the water and spotted the distorted shape of Deedee looking down at him. Motioning to Enrique that their task was hopeless, he kicked off for the surface.

'Gal?' demanded Deedee as he broke through into the air.

'I think I've got the fucking bends!' spluttered Gal.

He struggled to the side of the pool and, heaving himself out, flopped exhausted on to the poolside tiles. He lay panting for breath like a beached whale.

'How did that happen?' asked Deedee, hardly believing her eyes at the sight of the disaster area that had been her lovely swimming pool.

'I was nearly killed, that's all,' ranted her husband. 'I was minding my own bee's wax when that thing comes rolling down the hill. Look at the wall! Look at my sunbed! I was *that* much—' he indicated a matter of centimetres with his fingers '—from getting killed!'

Gal saw that Deedee was finding his description of attempted GBH by boulder somewhat difficult to take in.

'I'm serious! You nearly came home to a squashed husband!' he finished, hoping for some sympathy or at least recognition of his near-death experience.

Gal went over to the small table which stood next to the obliterated sunbed and picked up his mobile phone. He handed it to Enrique, who was lying at the side of the pool, still recovering from his diving exertions.

'Here you are. Phone your mate,' commanded Gal.

'Who?' said Enrique, completely lost.

'Your mate with the breakdown truck.'

'Filipe?'

'I don't know. If that's his bleeding name, then yes, that's him, innit? Give him a bell and tell him we need him over here – pronto.'

Gal walked over to Deedee and kissed her while Enrique began dialling. It was clear that his wife was more annoyed than concerned.

'Don't worry about this, love. It's nothing. We'll get this sorted out in two seconds.'

Enrique was now speaking Spanish into the phone. Gal couldn't understand a word, but he hoped that the rate the boy was talking gave some indication as to the speed his problems would be sorted out. When he looked back at Deedee he could tell that she wasn't taking this at all well. Compliments, Gal decided. Distract her with a good old-fashioned compliment.

'That dress is nice. Did you buy it today?'

'I was wearing it when I left. You bought it for me.'

Bollocks.

'Did I? Oh, love, I'm sorry. This rock thing's done me right in. My head's all like that,' apologized Gal, gesturing a whirly kind of confusion with his hand. 'You look beautiful anyway.'

Gal turned back to Enrique.

'Tell him he's going to need a winch or something if he wants to lift that,' he called.

'A what?'

Gal mimed the turning motions of a winch.

'A winch! Wincho! A fucking winch!' he articulated, getting more irate every second.

'All right, calm down,' soothed Deedee, suddenly concerned for Gal's blood pressure.

'Sorry, love. What a day I've had. I mean, to find out that at any moment a bloke could be crushed to death in his own back garden – 's just not right. The size of that fucker!'

Deedee gently squeezed Gal's shoulder, then walked slowly towards the house.

Enrique finished using the mobile and switched it off.

'Is he coming now?'

'Saturday,' shrugged Enrique.

'Saturday? Fucking Saturday?' exploded Gal. 'That's almost a week. That's no fucking good! You're useless, bleeding useless. Saturday! Saturday is …'

'Gal!'

From inside the kitchen, Deedee's firm voice cut short his tirade.

'Saturday,' muttered Gal quietly under his breath, 'I dunno. What's this bleeding country coming to?'

3. Night life

The hills lay in total darkness around Gal's villa. The only visible lights anywhere were the candles and lanterns which cast a warm glow over the patio. Somewhere, a CD player was letting 'Quiereme mucho' drift gently into the night.

Gal stood by his black metal barbecue, proudly in charge of the cooking. Nearby, Deedee and Jackie were sitting together at a patio table. They were both holding a glass of champagne in one hand and a cigarette in the other. Deedee was wearing a low-cut black dress that showed off her figure to full effect. Every time she sipped at the wine, or laughed, or leaned in to flick her ash, the silky material slid sensuously over her body's curves. Gal was having trouble concentrating on his duties as chef.

Aitch had left the little group and – rather worryingly in Gal's opinion – had wandered down to the assaulted swimming pool. He was now leaning down and looking deep into the clear water. In the four or so hours since the incident, the water level in the swimming pool had already fallen by one metre, exposing the tip of the invading boulder to the night air.

Gal kept attending to the barbecue although he was fully

aware that Aitch was circling the swimming pool intent on taking the piss. Aitch could smell a potential wind-up from half a mile away.

'Cor, it's done a fair bit of damage there, Gal. It's cracked the tiles,' observed Aitch, with mock innocence.

'I had noticed,' said Gal quickly. He desperately tried to stay calm, to concentrate on the sizzling barbecue in front of him.

'I'm not sure, but I think you might be losing a few inches of water somewhere as well,' continued Aitch, pointing towards the half-drained swimming pool.

Behind Gal, the two girls exploded into suppressed giggles.

'I could be wrong,' added Aitch, playing to the audience.

Hot fat from the barbecue splattered up the exposed part of Gal's arms, stinging him as he turned over a piece of meat.

'So when's that getting fixed then?' asked Aitch.

'Saturday apparently,' said Deedee, leaning across the table to refill Jackie's glass.

'I doubt it!' said Aitch, firmly.

'That Filipe geezer's coming over to take care of all of it. He's taking the boulder out on Tuesday, then coming to redo the tiles on Saturday. I hope,' confirmed Gal.

'Couldn't he do it no sooner?' questioned Aitch.

'Apparently, no, he bleedin' couldn't. OK?'

'No need to get touchy,' said Aitch, raising his hands in a gesture of friendly surrender.

Gal picked up a small tin of lighter fuel and pointed it at the red-hot coals under the barbecue's steel cooking grate. He squeezed it, but nothing happened, so he squeezed it harder. A stream of liquid suddenly erupted from the nozzle and hit the coals, sending a dense ball of flame whooshing into the air. Gal jumped back, slightly alarmed.

'Fucking hell!'

'Are you all right, darling?' asked Deedee, suppressing another smile.

'Yeah, I'm all right. Fucking thing.'

'He should be in a circus, he should. Gal Dove and his barbecue of death. He's a menace,' chuckled Aitch, finally leaving the poolside and returning to Gal and the girls.

'We're nearly ready,' said Gal, beginning to prod sausages and hamburgers on to a large plate.

Aitch sat down near the table and looked thoughtfully in the direction of the swimming pool.

'So when it's all fixed up, you gonna stick with the same colour water or what?' he suddenly asked Gal.

'How d'you mean?' said Gal, puzzled.

'The new water for the pool. You sticking with the plain?' said Aitch, deadpan.

'I dunno what you're talking about.'

'These days you can have different colours, can't you?'

'Fuck off!' was Gal's response.

The two girls were trying hard to keep a straight face, but they were both fighting a losing battle.

'Straight up! I'm telling you,' insisted Aitch. 'You can have different coloured water! I read about it in some of those poncy home-design magazines that our Jackie's always getting. Apparently it's all the rage in France.'

'Bollocks.'

'You can get a whole range of colours designed to suit your inner mood. Aquamarine, deep blue, mid-blue, tangerine – that could look nice in yours, go with the hearts. Lilac, indigo, pink, or just the old-fashioned plain. Anything you want,' explained Aitch patiently.

'Will you shut up?' asked Gal.

'You go to any of those DIY places in town. They've got a chart.'

'Is that right? I just have to go in and ask, do I?' said Gal, grabbing a plate off the pile at the side of the barbecue.

'Just ignore him, Gal,' advised Jackie, through a wide grin.

'But it's true, I'm telling you. At least check it out, have a look at the range. Some very famous scientists probably spent months cooped up in a laboratory somewhere inventing this and you don't even care.'

'Gal, he's just at it,' said Jackie.

'I'm not. What d'you mean? *At* what? I'm just trying to give some helpful advice,' protested Aitch. 'I'm trying to widen Gal's bleeding cultural experience.'

Gal passed Jackie a plate loaded with flame-charred meat.

'Aitch?' he said.

'Yes?'

'Do fuck off!'

'Is your man on drugs or something?' said Deedee to Jackie.

'He's losing it,' agreed Jackie, laughing.

Gal continued dishing out the food in stormy silence.

'Shut up, you. Ask yourself this, Gal. Why would I choose to lie about it, eh? *Why* would I?' reasoned Aitch.

'To wind me up like you always do!' bellowed Gal.

'If you want to think that, you think it!' huffed Aitch, turning away.

'I will!'

'Look, Gal, just have the fucking plain! Be old-fashioned. Fall behind.'

Gal held out a plate stacked with food.

19

'Shut up and have a sausage, will you?'

For a moment Aitch seemed hypnotized by the strange sight of the boulder half-submerged in the swimming pool.

'I wonder what started it moving,' he said quietly.

'Aitch?'

He looked up.

'What?'

'I said have a bleeding sausage, will you?'

Aitch took the plate from Gal and began to eat his way through the pile of goodies that were loaded on the platter.

'Tasty,' he said, mouth full of garlic bread and hamburger.

Gal watched his wife and friends eating and drinking and laughing, and drinking more. He watched Aitch attempt his infamous cigarette trick which involved him catching a lit fag in his mouth. The only thing wrong with Aitch's trick was that he couldn't fucking do it. One cigarette hit him on the forehead, another on the nose.

'You know you can't do it!' shouted Gal, growing more and more delighted with every failure. 'You know you can't!'

He watched Aitch never give up. He saw him drink more, and laugh more, and go through half a packet and still not give up. Until finally, with just two cigarettes left, he watched as Aitch flipped a lit fag and perfectly caught the end of it between his lips. Gal watched with joy as Aitch suddenly realized he'd caught the wrong end – the hot end. Gal watched him suffer the pain and raise his arms in triumph as he did a victory lap around the swimming pool anyway. Just for the hell of it.

Gal watched Jackie sitting perfectly content and smiling on their rough garden wall. Her long blonde hair was framed by the dark, shimmering leaves of the trees behind her, and her face was lit by fireflies dancing around her.

Most of all, Gal watched his wife Deedee. He watched her nuzzle her champagne glass softly against her lips. He watched her moving slowly around the patio, swinging her hips in time to the music. He watched her breasts push hard against her tight black dress, keeping their own undulating rhythm as she swayed back and forwards.

Gal watched this beautiful creature who – he still got a thrill when he thought of it – was *his* wife. He sat transfixed by Deedee while he lit a large cigar. She danced on, shaking her body, stamping her feet.

He watched nothing but Deedee for what seemed like hours. Then, taking a puff of his cigar, he leaned forward and exhaled a perfect heart-shaped smoke ring in her direction.

Deedee fixed him with a single, knowing look and walked purposefully towards him, passing through the smoky heart. She pressed her lips to his. Gal seemed to be suddenly weightless, floating somewhere between his villa and heaven. He was sailing high above the rooftop, drifting across the starry sky, held only by the touch of Deedee's lips.

It was clear the evening's hospitality was over. Aitch and Jackie discreetly made their exit, and Gal and Deedee retired inside.

Anticipating the pleasures still to come, Gal took one last look at the moon and stars through his bedroom window.

Yeah, roll on Saturday, that's what I say. Every morning then, twenty-five lengths before breakfast without fail. It's gonna be invigorating. I'm going to get a whole new regime going and stick to it. Get motivated. Swimming's the best thing ... next to Special K, I suppose ...

Suddenly Gal's musings were interrupted as he heard an

unmistakable moan of pleasure coming from the bed. His attention snapped back into the room.

'Bloody hell, Dee. Have you started without me?'

Gal stared hungrily over to the bed and the dark shape gently writhing beneath the coverlet.

'What are you doing to me? Oh, don't do that, I love that!' he protested, hurriedly dropping his gold and black kimono to the floor.

'I love you. I really love you, Deedee,' Gal said as he pressed his body against his wife's.

'Yeah?'

'I love our life here. I love us.'

All things considered, it was a shame that it was all about to go straight to hell.

4. 'Are you trying to say that you think I'm a cunt?'

It was raining, of course. It was always raining in London these days. Big Dave paced up and down the hallway of the house, stealing regular glances through the glass of the front door. The bare wooden floorboards creaked with every step he took.

The semi-derelict building was Dave's safe house, hidden deep within an ugly and unpleasant part of Stoke Newington. A movement outside caught Dave's attention and he looked up in time to see two strapping teenagers sprinting along the street, holding what looked like some poor bastard's car stereo.

Sitting alone and shivering in the back room of Dave's house, Terence Deary was not a happy bunny.

He was sitting on a threadbare armchair; thick masking tape bound his arms at the wrist to the arms of the chair. His ankles were also bound, making any movement impossible, while a patch of masking tape covered his mouth, leaving just enough of his nose clear to let him breathe. His face and thick black beard were caked with dried blood from a deep gash on his forehead.

Dave peeked through the door into the darkened room where Terence was trussed up. The captive's eyes were white and moist with panic, a bit like a pig's waiting for the farmer's knife.

'This might be him,' said Big Dave, hearing a car pull up at the front of the house.

Before Dave could reach the front door, it burst open and Don Logan marched into the hall.

'Where?'

'Back here, Don. All nice and safe like you wanted,' Dave told him.

Don strode into the back room. Terence's eyes widened with fear as the man appeared in the doorway.

Don Logan was a small, compact man, completely bald with a dark goatee beard. He moved with a quiet fury which could explode without warning.

'Hello there, Tel,' said Don, in a quiet, calm voice. 'I understand you've been a naughty boy with a photocopying machine? Is that right?'

Terence did his best to plead his innocence through the masking tape gag.

'Shut up, you cunt!'

Don moved back to the doorway where Big Dave was waiting and leaned close to Dave's ear.

'Go and get me something from the garden,' he whispered.

Big Dave looked scared and puzzled in equal measure. Unable to stand Don's stare any longer, he headed towards the back door.

Don returned to his prisoner and leant down in front of him.

'I thought that I could rely on you, Tel-boy. There's me, getting a little job together, few good lads. Gotta be good lads. Had you down for the driving. You're a nice little driver – good, safe, never get pulled over. And then what fucking happens?'

Don stood up, his voice erupting into pure rage.

'I'll tell you what fucking happens. I get a phone call right in the fucking middle of *Who Wants to Be a Millionaire* saying, "Oh, sorry to disturb you, Don, but Tel's been copying all the plans for the job. We found them at his place. Now, why would he have those fucking building plans there? Could you come and have a little chat with him?"'

Don dropped down close to Terence's face.

'So I said, "But Tel is a good lad. He wouldn't be thinking about shopping his friends." You weren't thinking about shopping your friends, were you, Tel?'

Tel shook his head violently.

Don balled his fist and brought it smashing down on Terence's face. There was the crack of teeth breaking and Terence began to cough.

'Don't start messing about, Tel.'

Bound by the masking tape, Terence was forced to gulp down a mouthful of his own blood and teeth.

'I think you're a cunt, Tel, and I won't have cunts working for me. Why should I have cunts working for me, eh? Can you tell me that?' shouted Don, leering over the terrified man.

Big Dave appeared in the doorway dripping with rainwater. In his hand was a small plastic hand trowel. He looked just as confused as when he had left.

Don walked slowly over, and took a closer look at the trowel which he could now see had a small blue train running along its handle with the words 'Thomas the Tank Engine' next to it. Don leaned close to Dave's ear and spoke quietly.

'Dave, are you trying to tell me that you think I'm a cunt?'

Dave moved back.

'No, Don ... Not at all, Don. No.'

'Go outside and get me a proper tool. For *him*,' said Don, nodding his head towards Terence.

Dave ran for the back door and returned in a few moments with a large metal shovel. This time Don took the heavy metal tool eagerly.

'Nice.'

Then he went into the back room and closed the door behind him. Unsure of what to do next, Dave waited by the door, taking up a kind of sentry duty.

'Are you fucking trying to wind me up?' he could hear Don bellowing through the door. 'I'm planning a job, and you're copying the details and taking them home? Do you think I'm going to let you get away with that? Do I look fucking stupid to you? *Do* I?'

Dave heard the sound of metal hitting bone and guessed that it was a knee.

'Who were you gonna fucking call, Tel? Fucking *Crimewatch*?'

In the hallway, the sound of further awful blows issued through the closed door. It was the sound of Terence Deary's skull being gradually cracked open one blow at a time.

Don Logan was enjoying himself, in his own, unique way.

Another noise made Dave jump and he realized that his pocket was playing the 1812 Overture. He fished out his mobile phone – it was a welcome distraction from the sickening crunches in the next room.

As Dave finished his call, Don emerged from the room, still holding the shovel.

'Look at that,' he said proudly, gesturing towards the blade.

Dave studied the bits of bloodied hair and bone fragment on the spade, unsure of what he should be looking for – yet trying to seem keen.

'Not even dented, that is,' explained Don. 'That's proper British craftsmanship for you. No foreign rubbish – Sheffield steel, that is.'

He thrust the shovel towards Dave.

'And get rid of him, will ya?'

'Yes, Don.' Dave glanced inside the room and quickly wished he hadn't.

Don was already marching down the hallway towards the front door. 'And if someone won a million pounds tonight and I've fucking missed it, I shall be most put out,' he threw back over his shoulder.

'There was a call on my mobile while you were … occupied,' Dave called after him quickly. 'Some woman saying that your airline ticket is ready. Where you off to, Don? I though we had a job.'

'Spain,' shouted Don, opening the front door into the grim windswept night. 'And I fucking hate Spain.'

Don slammed the door behind him, leaving Dave staring down at the shovel, adorned with its sticky mess of bone and hair.

'Why fucking Spain?' Dave wondered, but it was too late. Don Logan was gone.

Gal was sweating again – sweating like a pig. He was trudging across the hillside under a baking noon sun. A shimmering heat haze wobbled the distant landscape surrounding him. Gal was wearing cut-off denim shorts, a combat vest and huge walking boots. He was carrying a backpack and around his body was strapped enough provisions to feed twenty people for a week. By his side was Aitch, who was considerably less laden and looking much the happier for it. Strapped across Aitch's shoulder was his brand-new Winchester rifle.

'My new cowboy gun!' he had proudly proclaimed to Gal as they set out that morning.

Aitch was determined to put Enrique in his place once and for all and show him how hunting and shooting was really done.

Walking ahead of them was Enrique, with his father's rifle held proudly in his hands ready for action. Enrique's keen eyes scanned the dusty hillside for their prey – hares.

'I think you're being a bit harsh there, Gal,' Aitch was saying. 'It's not that bloody bad!'

'Yeah? Then you name me one thing that you miss. Name me one thing that you can't get here,' demanded Gal.

'Well, there's snooker. Can't play snooker here.'

'You could if you bought a table and had it shipped over. What else?' said Gal, dismissively.

'Well ...' Aitch realized his argument was running out of steam. 'I don't know. Galleries, museums, the river.'

'Museums? Last time you and me was in a museum, I was casing the joint, if you remember. When do you ever go to museums?'

'That's not the bloody point. They're there if you want them.'

'They're there if you wanna bloody rob them, you mean. Anyway, they do have museums here, as well you know,' explained Gal.

'Yeah, but it's not the same. Different culture, different things,' said Aitch, pulling a sour face.

'But I'm not asking you if it's different. 'Course it's bleeding different. I'm asking you what do you actually, really and truly miss about London?' said Gal, his voice rising.

'I miss lots of things,' said Aitch, with a shrug.

'Like fucking *what*? *Name* one!' shouted Gal.

'Snooker.'

Gal, walked away, utterly exasperated.

'Cunt,' he said simply, under his breath. 'You know you don't really miss anything.'

Gal suddenly stopped dead and signalled to Aitch to do the same. Twenty feet in front of them, Enrique had seen something move and now he was taking aim with his gun. Gal glanced across at Aitch with a look of sympathy.

The barrel of Enrique's gun was covered with ancient rust. The sights were very obviously not aligned and, most worrying of all, there seemed to be some important-looking pieces of the weapon missing.

'He ain't gonna hit fuck-all with that blunderbuss!' insisted Aitch.

'Sshh!' hissed Gal. 'Give the kid a chance.'

'He'd be better off with a spear!'

'Will you shut up!' whispered Gal, loudly.

The men watched as Enrique's finger tightened around the trigger, his face a mask of intense concentration.

'I'll give you 100–1 against!' whispered Aitch, unsupportively.

As Enrique tugged at the trigger, the hare suddenly became aware of the men's presence and darted for cover. Panicking, Enrique jerked his finger.

The ancient weapon's tired internal mechanism moved sluggishly into life. The gun clicked, then made a painful grating sound as it emitted a wisp of grey smoke. Finally, as if to add insult to injury, a spinning dum-dum bullet leapt lifeless from its rusting barrel and fell to the ground.

The hare was long gone.

Behind Enrique, Gal and Aitch roared with laughter.

'*Bastardo!*' screamed Enrique at his own gun. Then he noticed his companions nearly doubled up with laughter and understood that it was entirely at his expense.

'Shut up, Aitch, shut up!' Enrique cursed, marching away from his tormentors.

'That was a sitting duck! How could you miss that!' Aitch called after him.

When Gal and Aitch were once again able to stand, the trio continued their trek across the Spanish countryside. After a while, Aitch broke into the beer rations – only one bottle each allowed until they actually killed something.

'Anything, just as long as it's dead.'

Climbing over a rough stone wall, they began to cross a bumpy field, its dry grass shrivelling under the sun. Unable to complete any activity in silence for long, Aitch began to share the benefit of his shooting experience with Enrique.

'You gotta squeeze the trigger, pal. *Squeeze* it! You're always pulling at it, jerking it!' insisted Aitch.

Enrique was well pissed off.

As they came to a glade where the grass was thicker, Aitch stopped. 'Hold up,' he whispered urgently.

The trio stopped moving and in the clearing ahead saw a baby rabbit, no more than a few weeks old.

Aitch raised his Winchester.

'He's a little peach!'

Aitch took careful aim.

'He's only a tiddler, Aitch. Just a baby,' protested Gal.

'That's his problem, ain't it? Prepare to meet your maker!' murmured Aitch gleefully.

Gal could only watch as Aitch took careful aim. Years of bullying from others had put a cruel, cold streak into Aitch when it came to things smaller than himself.

Aitch smoothly eased down the gun's mechanism and heard the sound of a bullet shifting neatly into place inside the chamber. As he began to gently squeeze the trigger, the entire section suddenly came apart in his hands.

Aitch looked down, utterly shocked, while Gal and Enrique exploded into uncontrollable laughter.

Aitch could not believe it.

'Fucking thing!'

Gal collapsed to the ground, helpless.

'Cowboy gun? It's a bloody cowboy gun all right!' he managed to splutter through his hysterical tears.

5. My dinner with Gal

'I couldn't stand up for ten minutes. Aitch got so annoyed, it was lovely. It just fell apart. Enrique nearly wet himself,' explained Gal, not for the first time.

Gal, wearing a smooth beige suit and pale blue shirt, was sitting across from Deedee in one of their regular restaurant haunts. Smartly-dressed waiters in perfect white tops and crisp black trousers floated back and forth bringing ever more food from the hidden kitchen.

As usual, Gal was having trouble raising his eyes above Deedee's cleavage, much of which was on display on the opposite side of the table.

'He wouldn't have shot it, would he?' asked Deedee.

'I don't know. He can be a right cruel cunt at times, can Aitch. He might have. Still, he didn't get the chance, did he?' smiled Gal, remembering once more the sight of Aitch's gun falling apart.

Gal tore his eyes away from Deedee long enough to glance at the menu on the table in front of him. Deedee took a sip of her aperitif and aimed her sparkling eyes straight at Gal. He looked up just in time to catch a hint of a smile playing across her lips.

'What?' asked Gal, bashfully.

'Nothing. Just looking,' said Deedee.

Gal shifted uncomfortably in his seat and leaned forward.

'You'll give me a hard-on!' he warned.

'Yeah?' said Deedee, deliberately teasing him.

Gal stared at her longingly for a few more seconds before finally returning to the menu.

'I love it when you look at me, Deedee. I love being with you. What you fancy tonight, then? I'm having the calamari. What you gonna have?' asked Gal.

'I'm not sure yet,' said Deedee, still searching her menu for something special. 'Where's Jackie and Aitch? They should have been here by now.'

'I don't know, do I? Here, there's always mussels. You like mussels – have them?' suggested Gal, returning to his favourite subject of food.

'No, I think I'm gonna have that new chicken thing,' decided Deedee.

'Chicken thing? What new chicken thing? Where's that? I never saw that,' said Gal, alarmed in case he was missing out on something.

Hurriedly, he scanned the menu again and found the new chicken thing in the specials section. Then, reading the description, he immediately decided against it.

'Sounds disgusting – I hate melted cheese. You have that if you want. I'm gonna stick with the calamari. Shall we order? I'm bloody starving.'

'Here they are,' announced Deedee, seeing Jackie and Aitch finally making their way across the restaurant. 'Look at their faces. I hope they haven't had a row.'

Gal looked at the approaching figures and saw exactly what Deedee meant.

'Whatever it is,' said Gal as they reached the table, 'leave it outside, OK? We're here to have a nice evening, all right? Jackie, you look beautiful,' he finished, trying desperately to lift the mood.

'Can you get me a brandy, Aitch?' said Jackie, as she slid into her seat.

'That's what I like to hear. Brandy. Bloody brandy! I'll have one of those,' Gal enthused. 'I'm having the calamari. What do you want? Have that, you love that.'

Jackie couldn't bring herself to look at either Gal or Deedee and kept her eyes firmly on the table.

'Aitch, can you get me that brandy, please?' she said, quietly but firmly.

Deedee was getting worried.

'Are you all right, Jackie?'

'Tell them then, Jack,' said Aitch, reaching forward to pour himself a glass of red wine from Gal's bottle. Aitch poured the crimson liquid too quickly and spilled a little, blotching the white tablecloth with blobs of red.

'Tell me what?' said Gal, a clutch of icy fear beginning to form in his stomach.

'Are you definitely retired?' Jackie said slowly, regretting every word that came out of her mouth.

For a second, Gal looked relieved.

'Yeah, I'm retired. Why?'

'Definitely?' asked Jackie.

'I'm definitely bloody retired. What's this all about? How come I'm getting a sweat right up my back?' said Gal.

'Gal, we had a phone call, just before we left the house. That's why we were late,' continued Jackie.

'Yeah, and ... ?'

'And it was from London.'

34

Suddenly everything made sense.

'He's definitely retired,' cut in Deedee. 'Definitely.'

So that's what this was all about. Some old 'friend' had thought of Gal for a job, not realizing he was out of the game. Not realizing that he'd put all that shit behind him and had retired to the land of the shining sun.

'Wait a minute, love. Let's get this straight,' said Gal to Jackie. 'You got a call, the phone goes and it's a job, right? And they want me?'

'Yeah.'

'They don't want anyone else?'

'No.'

'They want Gal Dove? And they ask you to ask me, yeah?' said Gal, mustering his confidence again.

'Yeah.'

'All right – what's the problem? You've asked me, an' I've said no. I don't care what it is. I don't even wanna *know* what it is. I'm retired, and I'm saying no, so that's it. Why are we still talking about it?' he finished.

Gal looked over at Jackie to see if she was any happier now but she was looking at him with pity – like a vet about to put down a family pet.

'Jackie?'

'It was Don Logan,' she said quietly.

Perhaps she thought that saying it softly might make it less real, less true, less of a giant mind-fuck.

Silence.

Nobody at the table moved for several seconds … maybe days … it was hard to tell. Real mind-fucks are like that.

'It was Don Logan,' repeated Gal, suddenly seeming punch-drunk at the news.

'Oh Christ,' said Deedee, cradling her forehead in her hands.

'Gal, I'm sorry. I didn't know what to say to him. He said to ask you, so I had to ask,' pleaded Jackie.

'That's all right, Jack. That's all right, love. It's not your fault, honest. 'Course you had to ask,' Gal said, staring straight into space.

Gal knew this wasn't her fault. What else could the poor cow have done?

'Gal, I'm so sorry,' she said again.

Aitch looked at Gal's crumpled face, and his body, now slumping in his chair like a puppet whose master has cut its strings.

'You should never have picked up the fucking phone,' Aitch snarled.

'What's he doing calling you anyway? Why didn't he just call us?' wondered Deedee.

If there had been anyone at the table not in a state of deep and unpleasant shock, they might have spotted a guilty look bloom quickly, then just as quickly die, on Jackie's face – but they didn't.

Aitch came unknowingly to her rescue.

'Who knows what goes on in that cunt's head!' he said, expressing his complex opinion of Don Logan's psychological make-up.

Gal thought hard. He could handle this, couldn't he?

'You tell Don, from me – thanks for thinking of me, but I have to decline his offer. No offence, but I'm just not up for it, all right? Now let's drop the subject,' he reasoned.

Aitch looked uneasy. 'You can't tell him that.'

'Well then, you tell him that I'm tempted but I can't do it. Tell him I've lost my nerve. That I'd be no use to him at all. Just be a liability. Pity, my loss and all that,' offered Gal.

'Be serious, Gal,' pleaded Aitch.

36

Gal knew he was grasping at straws.

Don Logan. Fucking Don Logan – why did he have to call?

Gal swayed in his chair like a cornered animal.

'Well then, you tell him what the fuck you like, Aitch. You tell him anything. Anything. You all right there, Dee?'

Deedee's world had just fallen apart.

'Yeah, I'm fine,' she lied.

Gal drained the last of the liquid from his wine glass, then began again. 'What else did he say? Did he say anything else? How long did you talk to him?'

'He rates you, Gal,' said Aitch.

'Just that he wants you,' Jackie finished.

Gal needed another drink.

'Reckons there's no risk,' added Aitch.

Gal's eyes flashed with anger and Aitch realized that he'd just voiced the worst thing he could possibly have said.

'Can I have a beer, please,' snapped Gal to a passing waiter. Then he turned back sharply to Aitch. 'Well, I'm telling you that he can't have me. You tell Don that he can stick his fucking job right up his fucking hole.'

'You can tell him yourself,' said Jackie, sheepishly.

'What? He's coming over?'

Jackie swallowed hard. 'Yeah, tomorrow.'

'Bastard wants us to pick him up at the airport,' finished Aitch. 'Sorry, Gal.'

A bleak silence settled over the table. Deedee didn't lift her eyes from the menu still in front of her. A waiter's arm appeared between Gal and Deedee, unobtrusively slipping in a tall glass of beer. Sensing the brittle atmosphere, the waiter made a quick escape. Gal took a long drink.

'Nice beer, that, nice and cold. It's always nice here. I

love this restaurant. Deedee, my lovely wife. She's beautiful. I love my wife. I love you, Deedee,' said Gal, looking her straight in the eyes. 'Come Saturday I'll have my swimming pool back and I can swim in it again. I used to dream of that, I used to dream of this life. Guess where? That's right, inside. In the bloody nick. I'd picture myself with Deedee by a pool, somewhere really hot. Fat, drinking beer ...'

Gal took another deep swig. 'I used to visualize it every night. I could see it, fucking real, and now it's happened. We're here. We're all here. "No risk!" he says. No fucking risk. I've heard that before! Nine fucking years of my life I lost. No fucking risk!'

Gal grabbed the menu from the table and gave it a last look.

'Who's having what then? I'm having the calamari. What you having, Aitch?'

But it seemed that everyone had suddenly lost their appetites.

6. Hare today, Gal tomorrow

Gal wasn't sure where he was any more, but he knew it was hot. It was drop-dead, baking hot. He seemed to be in the middle of a desert. The sunbaked terrain stretched as far as he could see, empty and vast in every direction.

Gal was sitting at a table on which was a huge plate of perfectly cooked calamari. A small bowl of his favourite sauce waited at the plate's side, and the scent of warm lemon juice and herbs rose from the calamari's succulent brown batter. Gal lifted a piece to his mouth and took his first bite.

Without being told, Gal knew that something was approaching in the distance. He put another piece of calamari in his mouth and focused his eyes on a small black shape just visible through the distant heat haze. The black blur gradually transformed itself into the shape of a figure riding a donkey. The animal moved with a slow, lazy, humping motion – as if the walk was almost too much effort.

Gal ate another piece.

As the rider drew nearer, Gal saw without any surprise that the figure on the donkey was a six foot tall man-sized hare. Its hairy, bare-topped body was repulsive to look at.

Its long ears were distinctly suffering from a touch of mange, and the left ear had a large piece missing from its end.

Gal inserted another piece of calamari into his mouth, and ate it even faster than the last.

The creature was stooped, as if it had a humped back, and it wore silver-studded Mexican trousers, ending in Cuban-heeled boots. A band of intrepid flies hovered around its louse-infested head.

Gal decided that its name was Herman.

'Hello, Herman,' said Gal inside his head. His mouth said nothing – it was too busy chomping at a frantic pace.

The hare-man awkwardly dismounted from the donkey and stood staring at Gal. Gal ate faster. The hare-creature's stare was the vindictive, hate-filled gaze of a wronged friend. Its bloodshot man-rabbity eyes narrowed unforgivingly. Its whiskery mouth twitched, revealing yellow-stained and chipped teeth.

Gal didn't hear anything, but somehow he knew that in its head the monstrous hare had two voices, both gruff and both dark. In his mind the hare was repeating the words 'Guerras, Pestes, Hambres e Incendios,' over and over and over and over, and it was scaring the shit out of Gal.

He did the only thing he could to protect himself from the creature – he ate another piece of calamari. He was safe as long as he kept eating. Just keep eating.

From a saddle-holster on the donkey, Herman extracted an Uzi – one of the deadliest automatic weapons in the world. Herman cocked the safety catch.

'Caso Raro! Una mujer que dio a luz tres ninos y cuatro animales!' screamed the monstrous hare-beast.

Gal didn't understand a word of it; he just added another piece of calamari to the others. He was still chewing on the *gristly white flesh when the first bullets smashed into the table. They shattered the salt cellar and took large chunks out of the table's wooden surface. The ground seemed to be shaking with an Uzi-inspired earthquake.*

Gal grabbed his bottle of beer and tucked it under his arm for safe keeping. He stuffed another piece of food in his mouth. Then another and another.

A hail of well-aimed bullets cut clean through one of the legs of the table and Gal found himself having to support it with his spare hand and knee.

He reached to his plate to pick up another piece of his beloved calamari, but the plate was suddenly empty. Herman replaced the clip of ammunition in his Uzi and prepared to fire again.

Gal jolted awake and found himself in bed covered in a hot, sticky sweat. The first thing he noticed was the empty space in the bed next to him where Deedee should have been. By the purple half-light filtering through the windows, Gal could tell that there was still a while to go before dawn.

He quickly got up and grabbed his dressing gown. Slipping it over his naked torso, he headed downstairs to find his wife.

Deedee was sitting outside by the edge of the swimming pool. She sat utterly motionless, watching the last of the water draining away through the cracked tiles.

Gal hurried over to her, putting his arm around her shoulders. The pre-dawn chill had made her flesh cold to the touch.

'What you doing down here? You all right, darling? What is it? Come back to bed,' whispered Gal, softly.

'I'm not tired,' said Deedee. What she really meant was that she couldn't sleep.

'No, neither am I, but come on,' Gal said, giving her arm a gentle tug. Deedee didn't move.

'Look, it's gonna be all right. It'll be OK,' tried Gal, sounding unconvincing even to himself.

Deedee looked across at him and then quickly turned away again.

'What? Look, what's the worst thing that can happen? What's the worst-case scenario? He's gonna come here – ask me – I'm gonna say no. He's not gonna like it, but what else can he do? Then he's gonna leave,' promised Gal.

Deedee didn't share her husband's optimistic vision of such an encounter.

'That simple?'

'Yes, that simple. I'll tell him "No" to his face, then he'll go. Now, please come back to bed. I miss you.'

Deedee's eyes came to rest on the shattered tiles at the bottom of the pool.

'Why does it have to be you?'

'Because the man is a cunt, pardon my French,' said Gal. 'And that's what cunts are like – that's why they're cunts and the rest of us aren't. I don't know why me. You'd have to find another cunt and let him tell you, because I just don't know.'

'I've been thinking – we don't have to be here,' Deedee said, tentatively.

'Now that would be the wrong thing to do and you know that. That would be like a red rag to a bull!' said Gal.

He knew that, however attractive the idea of packing and running might seem, it would be the worst thing they could do. Don Logan might just take a firm no for an answer, but legging it would just be an open invitation for him to come after you. And Don had contacts everywhere. He'd find you sooner or later, and he wouldn't be best pleased when he did.

'He's coming, that's the situation and there's nothing we can do about it. I don't like it any more than you, but there we are. I'll tell him to his face that I'm not interested. That's all I can do. There is nothing else.' Gal looked intently at Deedee. 'And you know that I'm not interested, not one per cent, and that's what I'm gonna tell him tomorrow. Now come here and give us a hug.' He stretched his arms wide.

Deedee went quickly to him and nuzzled forcefully into Gal's chest.

'Who am I?' said Gal, pressing Deedee's body tightly against him.

'My big-bear-man, Jabambo,' she answered in a small, scared voice.

'That's right, you remember that. You trust me,' said Gal, seeing that Deedee was close to tears.

'He'll hurt you.'

'Me? Nah! Not me! He can't hurt me, can't hurt Jabambo!' Gal answered in the bravest voice that he could muster. But in his heart, he knew exactly what Deedee was referring to and it cut him to the core.

'He can. You know he can. I'm warning you. He'll use it,' warned Deedee.

'I don't give a monkey's what he says, and neither should you,' announced Gal, 'Let him say what he wants. We're big enough to take it! We're a team. He can't beat us, can he?'

Deedee pushed herself back from Gal's chest and looked deep into his eyes.

'Do you love me, Gal?'

Of all the questions she could have asked, of all the 'what ifs' she could have posed, this was the simplest question that

43

Gal could have had to answer. It was so simple and so obvious that it almost took him by surprise.

'How can you ask me that?' he spluttered. ''Course I love you, 'course I do. With all my heart. God, I love you so very much – I don't think you understand how much. It's fucking huge, my love for you.'

He drew Deedee towards him once more and folded his arms right around her.

'Do I love you? I've heard everything now! Bloody cheek!' he finished.

Deedee raised a hand to his face and said, 'I love you, Gal, I love you so much.'

The first light of dawn began to peek over the distant mountains as they began to walk back to the house, arm in arm.

'You can only feel sorry for people like Don. Now, come on – let's try and get some kip,' suggested Gal.

He closed the kitchen door behind them, leaving only an empty patio and waterless pool to greet the new day.

7. The cunt now arriving at Gate 14 . . .

Due to a strike by French air traffic controllers, the cunt in question was two hours late arriving at the airport. Aitch and Jackie arrived there exactly on time and had to drink endless cups of tasteless coffee in the airport café while they waited for Don's aircraft to be rerouted via Switzerland.

When the plane finally arrived, Jackie and Aitch watched it taxi across the runway and come to a stop near the small terminal. As the doors opened, they caught sight of Don Logan pushing his way past the staff to be the first passenger off. He'd obviously had more than enough of in-flight hospitality.

'There he is. The cunt.'

Don's hairless head glowed with the reflected rays of the morning sun. He was dressed in grey trousers and black Chelsea boots. He carried his jacket in one hand, while his short-sleeved white shirt revealed the tattoos on both forearms. Aitch knew what they were without looking. So did Jackie – for entirely different reasons.

On his right forearm was a faded blue and green tattoo of a wild panther, posing mid-spring. On his left arm was a pair of crossed hammers, together with the letters 'WHU' – for Don's beloved West Ham United.

Don took quick, purposeful strides along the airport concourse towards Aitch and Jackie.

'Hello, Don,' said Aitch, over-keenly.

'I've seen the fucking Alps,' announced Don, marching straight past them. Aitch and Jackie quickly scooted to catch him up.

'Did I ask to see the fucking Alps? No, I did-fucking-not. Bloody cheek, flying me over the bloody Alps,' continued Don, in a flat monotone.

'Still, they are beautiful, aren't they?' ventured Aitch.

Don stopped dead and Aitch only just avoided walking into him – a potentially fatal mistake.

'They're not beautiful if you don't wanna see them. They're not beautiful if you're dying for a dump and there's a queue for the toilet. They're not beautiful then, are they?' said Don, lowering his voice and staring at Aitch eyeball to eyeball.

'No, Don. I don't suppose they would be.'

'Shut up, Aitch,' ordered Don. 'Where's your car? You have got a car?'

'Yes, Don.'

'What did I just say?'

'Sorry, Don,' said Aitch, shutting up and signalling to Jackie to lead the way.

When they reached the car, Don automatically claimed the passenger seat next to Jackie and Aitch was relegated to the rear. Don and Jackie hadn't exchanged a word since he had landed, and since Aitch had been told to shut up, it was evidently to be a very quiet journey.

Aitch decided that so far, this visit was going just as badly as he had expected.

'It's coming!' shouted Gal.

Slowly but surely the boulder that had brought such calamity to Gal's swimming pool was being lifted. The offending lump of stone was encased in thick, steel chains which held it prisoner as if the monster rock might struggle, King-Kong-style, to escape. The chains were attached to the huge, rusty winch on the back of Filipe's ancient truck, now parked by Gal's poolside.

'Keep taking it, it's coming,' yelled Gal, imagining that Filipe could hear him over the din of the winch.

Gal was down in the pool, guiding the rock on its upward journey, while Filipe, fat and oil-stained, sat in the safety of his truck working the winch controls. Enrique stood at the edge of the pool with a large grin on his face, as if he were in charge of the proceedings.

The boulder touched down on the rear of the truck with a harsh clang. In the pool, Gal kicked away a few of the loose tiles with his foot and inspected the damage. Not good. Then he climbed out of the pool and went over to Enrique, pulling a wad of money from his pocket and giving the notes to the boy.

'Here you are, sort him out. He can have the balance on Saturday once it's retiled, all right?' said Gal.

'*Sí!* We take rock away now, but Filipe return to do tiles.'

Gal cast a glance around him to make sure that Filipe wasn't listening, then leaned down to the boy's eye level.

'Listen, son. Stay away from here for a bit. I'm all right for jobs for the moment.'

'What?'

Gal could see confusion and hurt in the boy's face.

'I'm all right. Don't need you for a bit, that's all.'

'Why? I do something wrong? Filipe no good?' asked Enrique.

'No, it's not that. It's none of your bloody business why, that's why! I've just got things to do. I'm gonna be busy. Now, go on – bugger off!' said Gal, seeing if a large smile would brighten the kid's mood.

Filipe revved up the truck's engine as Enrique climbed into the passenger seat. The boy slammed the door, then leaned out the window and called to Gal.

'Gal, fat bum, Gal!' shouted Enrique, giving Gal a huge grin and the middle finger as the truck drove off.

All, it seemed, was forgiven.

'Yeah, yeah, all right,' muttered Gal, watching them leave. Climbing back down into the empty swimming pool, he began sweeping up bits of broken tile with a dustpan and brush.

As Gal got to work, Jackie's silver Mercedes and its visitor from London were speeding along the highway, and was just about to take the dusty turning that led to Gal's villa. The journey had been a tortuous and awkward affair. No one had spoken, except Don, who broke the silence to remark how he didn't see why they had to drive on the wrong fucking side of the road out here.

Several times Jackie had caught Don stealing sideways glances at her legs and at her breasts. She felt a cold chill whenever she saw his eyes ogling, as if they were actually crawling over her body.

As they approached Gal's place, they passed the winch truck coming in the opposite direction. Leaning out of the window, Enrique saw the serious look on Jackie's and Aitch's faces, and strained to see who the stranger sitting in the passenger seat could be. Was he the reason that fatty Gal didn't want him around for a while? Enrique watched the car until it receded out of sight.

48

As Jackie pulled into the Doves' driveway, Deedee's face appeared at a window. In her heart, she was hoping that the bastard simply wouldn't show up. As Don Logan got out of the front of the car, she saw that her prayers for a plane crash had sadly not been answered.

Hearing the noise of the car's arrival, Gal stopped his work and climbed up the silver ladder at the edge of the pool. His face was suddenly flushed and his stomach was a mass of worry knots. Must be natural and relaxed, Gal kept telling himself. Must look casual.

Don walked quickly from the car towards the villa.

'Gotta change my shirt, it's sticking to me,' he said, ignoring Gal completely. 'I'm sweating like a cunt.'

Don marched upstairs.

'The guest room's the second on the right, Don,' called out Gal, as the man disappeared up the stairs.

A few minutes later, Don came back downstairs wearing a fresh shirt, though not looking any more sociable.

'That's fucking better,' he said, taking a large whisky from Gal.

Don sat down in the lounge, while the other four gathered around him. The girls kept their eyes firmly rooted on the floor, as Gal and Aitch frantically tried to think of something to say. Of anything to say.

Silence.

'How's things at home, Don?' tried Gal eventually, somewhat desperately.

'We're ninth on goal difference. Last week we lost 2-1 to Southampton. Fucking Southampton. Fucking own-goal in the last minute. I couldn't believe it. I said to Terence Deary – he was in the pub with me – that I couldn't fucking believe it.' Don gulped back half his whisky, as if that proved just how much he couldn't fucking believe it, before continuing.

'Next week, it's Barnsley at home. Goalie only breaks his bleeding leg in the twentieth minute. Reserve goalie comes on, he's about fourteen years old, isn't he? Suddenly we're down 4-2. We have three certain penalties turned down, and then we come back and win 5-4. That Harry Redknapp wants shooting. He's a good manager, I reckon, but he still wants shooting,' Don decided.

Silence.

'How is Terence?' said Aitch.

'He's been better,' said Don, remembering his last view of Terence – of a hole in Tel's skull.

Silence.

'How's your brother, Don?' piped up Aitch, quite pleased with the question he'd thought up.

'Malky? He's all right, I suppose. He's Malky, isn't he? I don't know. You'd have to ask him how he was.'

Malky was Don's brother and close enough in looks to be his twin. He had the same temperament as Don, so at any given moment it was always a good bet that the brothers were not speaking to each other.

'You patched things up?' said Aitch.

'It's up to him, innit?' said Don, with a casual take-it-or-leave-it shrug of his shoulders.

Silence.

Deedee's eyes caught Gal's and urged him to come up with something – anything.

'How was the flight, then, Don?' asked Gal.

Aitch flinched and prepared to hear Don's rant about his unwelcome detour over the Alps for a second time.

'Was all right,' said Don flatly, suddenly more interested in looking around the room. 'So, this is a Spanish villa, is it?'

Gal couldn't help smiling with pride.

'Yeah, this is it. The old 'acienda,' he gestured.

'It's a bit remote, isn't it? Bit cut off from the rest of the world?' said Don.

'No, it's perfect. It's not like we want –' Gal stopped himself saying 'many visitors' just in time '– er, want to be nearer the town. This is just how we like it. Do ya wanna have a look around?'

Don took another slug of his whisky.

'Yeah, I will in a minute. When I go for a piss.'

Aitch looked across at Gal, who gave him a small, barely noticeable nod.

'Right then, girls, you ready?' said Aitch, standing up and doing his best to fake casual ease. Jackie and Deedee jumped up from their seats in double-quick time and moved towards Aitch. Any reason to get away from Don. Any.

'Where you going?' demanded Don, his voiced laced with aggression and sudden resentment.

'Oh, I'm just taking the two ladies here out for something to eat. Thought we'd leave you two to it,' explained Aitch, locking eyes with Don.

'What, ain't I invited?' demanded Don.

Oh, Jesus.

'No, Don, 'course you're invited. 'Course you are! Only I thought you two might want some time to talk about things,' said Aitch, suddenly full of fear.

Don got up.

Please don't let him go mental.

A quarter of a smile played across Don's mouth.

'No, I'm only joking. It's all right – here you are, I'll get it,' offered Don, quickly slipping two fifty pound notes out of his back pocket and thrusting them at Aitch.

Aitch didn't know what to do.

'No, that's all right, Don. There's no need for that. You're our guest here. You shouldn't be paying.'

Don's face hardened.

Shit.

'Aitch, behave yourself. I'm paying for your meal, right?'

Behind Don, Gal urgently flashed his eyes at Aitch sending the message that he should, for fuck's sake, take the money.

Take the money and get out. Take the money and get out now, before it all goes wrong.

'Well, that's very kind of you, Don. Very nice of you,' said Aitch, accepting the notes. 'It's ...'

'Shut up,' ordered Don dismissively, sitting down again.

Deedee exchanged a goodbye look with Gal and followed Aitch and Jackie out of the house without another word. Deedee was feeling sick.

Gal saw the three of them climb into Jackie's car, and then watched through the window as she drove quickly away. When Gal turned around, he nearly jumped out of his skin because Don was right behind him; he'd been watching the women leave over Gal's shoulder.

'You nearly gave me a heart attack,' said Gal, trying to dredge up a smile.

'We wouldn't want that, would we?' said Don coldly. 'Shall we have a chat outside?'

Don walked towards the back door and Gal knew he had no choice but to follow.

8. 'I'm retired'

Of course the whole thing was a lie. Aitch and the others had no intention of eating – even if any of them had felt like it. Jackie drove the three of them back to her and Aitch's villa and, in silence, they shuffled inside.

Deedee knew that she had just left her beloved husband in the company of the biggest cunt that she had ever met in her entire life.

'Drink?' said Jackie. She handed Deedee a glass of whisky, showing that the offer hadn't actually been a question.

Aitch sank down on the sofa next to Jackie and looked at his watch. 'How long do we give them?' he said.

'Gal said wait till he calls,' said Deedee.

Aitch watched the second hand of his watch do one complete circuit. It was going to be a long fucking afternoon.

'We'll at least wait until sundown. If Gal hasn't called by the time it's dark, I'm going back anyway,' announced Deedee, draining her glass.

Aitch poured her another whisky and then went back to counting away the slowly ticking seconds.

As Don Logan stepped out of the Doves' back door, the first

thing that struck him was the totally baking, boiling, fuck-off, blazing white-heat of the sun. Blasting down from the noon sky, it felt like stepping into a laser beam.

'Fuck,' Don swore quietly to himself.

His eyes narrowed to thin slits as he strained to focus through the brightness. He held his hand up at different angles trying to shield his eyes, but nothing made any difference at all. Don could feel the heat like hot wax all over his completely bald head. He felt the sweat begin to prick out all over again.

Gal emerged from the kitchen door with two bottles of cold beer. He handed one to Don, then took a swig of his own.

'How long have we known each other? You and me?' asked Don, licking his lips.

Gal remembered very well the first time he'd ever seen Don. He was hardly likely to forget it. Gal had been sitting in a pub with some good old lads when a young man known as Madhouse Mikey had come hurtling through the pub window.

Don had asked Madhouse Mikey to step outside to settle a disagreement between gentlemen (i.e. have the shit kicked out of him) and had thrown Madhouse back into the pub. Mikey's shattered body had landed on their table, his bloodied head popping open Gal's bag of salt and vinegar crisps. Gal had never eaten another packet since.

'I don't know, Don. Fifteen years? Sixteen?' Gal finally offered, not anxious to get the right answer.

'Might be longer than that,' said Don, in his annoying monotone voice.

He took another long swig of beer. 'Fucking hell, it's hot, ain't it?' he complained, feeling that the heat was beginning to suck the life out of him.

'This is nothing, Don. It gets much hotter than this.'

'Strewth, it's unbearable! I don't know how you stand it. How do you stand it? It's far too bloody much,' said Don.

'You get used to it. I love it!' insisted Gal.

Don shook his head. 'No, it's too much!'

Out of the corner of his eye, Don saw a small brick in the garden wall begin to move. His eyes flicked it into focus and he saw that it had arms, legs, a tail, and protruding bug eyes. It moved with a blurred scurrying motion.

'What's that?'

'What?'

'That! There. That green thing running along on the wall – it's legging it!' said Don, more than a little alarmed.

'It's just a lizard. They're quite common out here. They're completely harmless. They just sit around eating flies all day.'

Don took a closer look and seemed to calm down as he watched the little creature suddenly freeze into a new insect-hunting position.

'Yeah? 'S quite nice, isn't it? Pretty colours. Anyway, that's not the reason I'm here,' said Don, surveying Gal's patio. 'Yeah, this is all right, isn't it? Not bad. What's that, then?' He pointed at Gal's waterless swimming pool.

'It's a swimming pool.'

'It's more of an empty bath, ain't it?'

'It's had a bit of an accident. We had a bloody big boulder come rolling down the hill. Just missed me by inches – I was nearly squashed. It broke some tiles – look,' said Gal, gesturing down to the empty depths.

But Don had already lost interest.

'Where is it they've gone, anyway?'

'Oh, some place that Jackie knows,' lied Gal. 'A couple

of miles up the road.'

'Nice?'

'Never been, but yeah, it's supposed to be.'

'You happy here?' said Don, curtly.

'Yeah. Very happy. It's what I've always wanted.'

Don scanned the hillside around them and sweeping brown landscape beyond.

'Bit out of the way,' he ventured.

'Nah, suits us. Get a bit of peace,' said Gal.

Don cast a quick glance at the villa. 'What's theirs like?'

'What, Jackie and Aitch's? They've got a smashing place. Loads of lovely bits and pieces. 'Course, we bought them together, same time like. It's just the right distance away. Not too near, so they're living in our pockets, but close – cosy like. Of the two I have to say I preferred ours. It's not just the location. It's the general feel. Feels more ...'

'More what?' said Don, a little too harshly.

'I don't know ...' said Gal, losing his train of thought. He could sense Don beginning to circle him like a shark. Soon he'd get to the point. Soon he'd ask.

'Yeah, I know what you mean,' Don agreed anyway. 'What did Jackie say?'

Gal felt his stomach lurch.

'Just that something was happening.'

Be careful.

'Which it is. And?' said Don.

Be very careful.

'Well, just that you were planning something.'

Don stared at Gal.

'Yeah?'

'Yeah,' shrugged Gal.

Don's beginning to turn the screw.

56

'And you said?'

'Well, I didn't say much. I just listened really. Mouth shut, ears open, you know.' Gal realized he was rambling and shut up.

'She put a question to you,' said Don.

'Yeah.'

Here it comes.

'Which was?' said Don.

'Well,' said Gal, making a deeply bad job of hiding his discomfort, 'that you'd thought of me.'

'To which you said ...?'

Avoid refusing to his face. Think of another way of saying it.

'Well, Jackie's probably told you what I said,' offered Gal, hopefully.

'She told me nothing,' shot back Don.

'Look, Don,' said Gal.

'*Look*, Don?'

Oh God.

'Don, look, it's like this ...'

'Like what?' pressed Don.

Bastard's gonna make it so hard.

'I'm ...'

'Mmm?' encouraged Don.

Tell him.

Oh God.

Tell him.

'Retired ...'

The word 'retired' seemed to hang in the air between them like a fart in a lift. Gal felt his body brace itself against the potential explosion of hate and bile, not to mention physical violence which he knew could erupt at any second.

'Are you?' said Don, simply and flatly.

Maybe give him a sweetener.

''Fraid so, Don. I've not got a lot of money, not a lot, but I've got enough and I'll do anything not to offend you, but I really can't take part. Thank you very much for the offer, but I'm just not up to it.'

'Not up to it? I see,' said Don.

Shit. He's getting stroppy.

'I couldn't do it, Don. I'd be useless to you,' shrugged Gal.

'Useless?'

'I would be. Yeah …'

'In what way?'

In any way. In every fucking way. Just let this end.

'In every fucking way,' said Gal rashly, then instantly regretting it.

Don took a step closer and peered directly into Gal's eyes.

'Why're you swearing? I'm not swearing. There's no need for swearing, is there?' asked Don, his voice hollow with politeness. He smiled thinly, then walked away from Gal, taking time to look around the patio and the view of the sweeping hillside around it.

'Sit down, Gal, and listen to a little story. Listen to me … listen to your Uncle Don, he's gonna tell you a little story. Y'see, I know a bloke, who knows this bloke, who knows a bloke …'

9. Anatomy of a bank job – Part I

This is the story that Don Logan told to Gal Dove.

It was a story of how Don had put together the job. It was a story with a lot of people in it and it went all over the bloody shop. Gal knew some of the names involved, others were unfamiliar. Sometimes Gal had to struggle to keep up. He listened hard, and tried to remember everything. Even when he wasn't sure what Don was saying, he nodded anyway.

But the worst thing wasn't keeping up with who said what. The worst thing was that with every word Don said, Gal could feel himself getting pulled in. With every detail he learned about the job, Gal felt himself getting drawn closer to it.

He didn't want to hear anything about Don's nice-earning, no-risk, maybe-another-nine-years-of-his-life, fucking bank job. But that didn't matter – he was going to hear about it anyway.

Don's story started when Don had been sitting watching television in the front room of his house in Chingford – the place he'd bought with a suitcase of cash in the early eighties. Don was watching a particularly slow half-hour of *Catchphrase*, the quiz show where cheery TV comic and all-round cheeky chappie Roy Walker invites cunts from the general public to solve various visual puzzles for money.

'Fucking too many cooks spoil the bollocks,' hissed Don under his breath, disgusted at the seemingly retarded nature of that week's ill-chosen contestants.

The telephone on the sideboard began to ring, interrupting Don's televisual pleasure.

Fucking hell.

Don let it ring several times.

Fucking, fucking hell.

'Do you wanna get that or what?' he shouted out, trying to aim his voice through the doorway and up the stairs.

'Get it yourself!' hollered Don's wife from the bedroom.

Don begrudgingly got up and, without taking his eyes off the TV screen (where the cunty retards had still not guessed correctly), picked up the phone.

'Hello?'

'Is that Mr Logan?' asked a quiet and deliberately threatening voice.

'Who's this?' said Don.

'Hello, Mr Logan,' said the voice.

'Hello.'

'What ya doing?' asked the mystery caller.

Who was this?

'I'm watching the telly,' answered Don.

'What ya watching?' continued the voice.

Don put a name to the voice.

'I'm watching *Catchphrase* ... Is that Stan Higgins?'

''Course it is, you cunt!' announced Stan, dropping the cloak-and-dagger voice. 'Listen, I might have something for you. Something big and juicy, yeah? You busy now? Meet me in the private bar downstairs at Faces, yeah? Park out the

60

back – you'll be all right.'

Don replaced the receiver without another word. He grabbed the remote control and smiled as he turned the television up to full blast before he left the house.

Stan Higgins was waiting for Don when he got to the otherwise empty bar. He was sitting at a table for two about as far away from the bar as you could get. He looked about fifty, was balding and wore amber-tinted spectacles – which no one had yet told him made him look like a pervert.

Don got himself a whisky and then listened to what Stan had to say as the two of them sat bathed in the red light of the bar's tacky illuminations.

'We need eight men, yeah? Strong lads who ain't afraid to graft. This one's gonna take all night. They've got to be good boys, all of them. Reliable – dead reliable, with positive attitudes. That's of the utmost importance. Essential,' insisted Stan. 'That's what we're looking for and I want you to put the team together, yeah?'

Don asked Stan who was behind the job.

'Who do ya think?' said Stan.

Don didn't know.

'Only Teddy.'

'Teddy Bass? Mr Black Magic himself?'

'Is there another Teddy?'

'How come?'

Stan settled down and told Don his story.

Teddy Bass was probably the most glamorous gangster in town. He lived in a luxurious riverside penthouse overlooking the Thames, with a glittering panoramic view over the whole city. His handsome, square-cut features and casual elegance were welcome almost anywhere on the London social scene.

'You know what he's like, old Teddy,' Stan explained.

'You know the circles that he moves in. Anyway, a few months back he was invited to this party at this massive place on The Bishop's Avenue. You know it?'

''Course, I bleeding know it.'

The Bishop's Avenue was one of the most famous addresses in London. Also known as Millionaires' Row, the road was home to numerous ambassadors, rich diplomats and minor members of foreign royal families.

'He was invited to a party there, but this gig turned out to be a wild party, right? A bloody orgy! He told me it was fucking incredible. Arses everywhere. Everyone doing the lot: wanking, spanking, fucking, cocaine, camcorders – you name it! It was like ancient fucking Rome!' explained Stan, with wild excitement in his eyes.

Stan told Don about Teddy's little adventure. How Teddy – surprised, but pleasantly so – began to take full advantage of the experiences being offered to him. How bare-chested Teddy was soon lost in the throes of the whole ecstatic-fantastic-electric experience. How his sweat-soaked hair whipped and lashed his brow as he dominated the room, his face contorting with pleasure, like a Minotaur about to come . . .

'Anyway, afterwards – and rather a long time afterwards, mind you – Teddy's taking five minutes to relax on the sofa. He's lying there, in the semi-darkness, in this expensively decorated room full of old tarts and ponces. Around him, barely discernible in the gloom, are some other "guests" in various states of undress. Most of them are too exhausted to even move, but their eyes are wandering round the room, pupils dilating, watching each other. Watching for tiny flickers of arousal.

'Teddy starts having a smoke, when this well-groomed

older man wanders in. He sits directly behind Teddy and starts kind of staring. Teddy keeps his eyes in front of him, where some old slapper with blonde hair called Jean is lying back in an armchair.

'"How are you feeling, Teddy? Are you all right? You having fun?" asks Jean.

'But Teddy doesn't really care because all he's bothered about is this new bloke and these eyes boring into the back of his head.

'"Yeah, it's a gas," says Teddy, then he turns around and says to the bloke, "What you staring at?"

'"The back of your head," says the bloke.

'"What did you say?" asks Teddy, all menacing and mean.

'"I'm staring," says the man, slowly and somewhat bored, "I'm staring at the back of your head."

'"Well don't. Stare at the back of your own fucking head," complains Teddy.

'The bloke just sits there, unimpressed, and kind of snorts – one of those posh you're-beneath-me little snorts. They obviously hadn't been properly introduced.

'The blonde tart steps in. "Harry, this is Teddy Bass. Teddy, this is Harry. Harry's the chairman of Imperial Emblatt."

'Now, maybe you've never heard of Imperial Emblatt. Why? Because they're a sniffy lot who don't need publicity and make sure that they don't get it. Bloody above all that, aren't they? Think of them a bit like Standard Grading in the late seventies – safety deposits boxes, only bigger. Much bigger.

'So, Teddy looks round at Chairman Harry again, and Chairman Harry stares right back at him, like he couldn't

63

give a toss.

'"Are you homosexual, Harry?" says Teddy.

'"Depends what you mean," says the Chairman, unfazed.

'This annoys Teddy because it was obvious what he meant.

'"Men or women?" asks Teddy, flatly.

'"Oh definitely," says Chairman Harry, dead keen. Then he gets up, takes hold of Jean's hand and leads her towards the door.

'"Is this a private party or can anyone join in?" calls out Teddy. The Chairman stops dead.

'"Said the man with the keyhole eyes," mutters the Chairman to himself, all snottily. Then he turns back to Teddy and says, "Feel free."

'Chairman Harry and Jean walk out the door, watched by Teddy whose hunger is suddenly coming back to him.

'"I'll have some of that," decides Teddy quietly, and follows the pair of them out. And that,' explained Stan, taking a final swig of drink, 'is how Teddy and the Chairman were ... shall we say, introduced.'

'Bloody hell,' said Don, simply. But he still didn't see where the story was going or how there was money in it for him.

'Get some more drinks,' said Stan, 'And when you come back, I'll tell you the really fuck-off part.'

10. Anatomy of a bank job – Part II

Don Logan returned from the bar with fresh drinks and put them on the table. Normally Don wouldn't buy a drink for Stan any more than he would spit on him if he was on fire, but if there was a job in it he always made an exception.

'Empty in here, ain't it?' said Don, sitting down again.

'That's because it's a right shit-hole,' said Stan kindly. 'That's why I like it.'

'Anyway ...' prompted Don.

'Anyway,' said Stan and continued his story.

'So now Teddy Bass and this Chairman Harry know each other quite well, as it were. Harry knows who Teddy is well enough, but he doesn't give a flying fuck – partly because he's one of those, "Aren't criminals wonderful and fascinating and misunderstood" types. But also because Harry's not as big a prick as he looks, as his particular safety deposit vault has got one of the most elaborate security systems in Europe. It's a fucking fortress, innit? There's nothing going in and out of that place ... except, that is, Teddy Bass.'

Stan told Don that Chairman Harry then invited Teddy into the very special Imperial Emblatt safety deposit vaults ...

Teddy arrived spick and span one morning in his Savile Row suit, black Oxfords and long, black coat. He took in every detail his eyes had time to eat up.

'Here's your personal key,' Chairman Harry told him, handing over a key labelled 'HS3671'.

'Thank you, Harry.'

'I'll leave you alone to make your deposit, obviously,' said Harry, guiding Teddy through the six-inch-thick, stainless-steel, high-tech security door that sealed the entrance into the actual vault.

Teddy waited for a few seconds as the hydraulic security door slid silently shut behind him. Then he walked down the ultramodern, pristine-condition corridor, lined on both sides with banks and banks of mirrored-steel safety deposit boxes.

Teddy's eyes flicked up to the security cameras mounted in each corner of the vault. There were four of them, covering every angle. He kept walking until he eventually came to Box HS3671 and stopped. Teddy inserted his key, gave it a double turn and opened the empty security box.

He reached into his pocket and, making sure that the cameras didn't see what it was, quickly put something into the box. It was an empty packet of Sullivan Powell cigarettes. (Well, Teddy wouldn't want to waste a full one, would he?) Then he shut the box, locked it and headed back down to the security door which began to open with a slow hiss.

Chairman Harry thought that Teddy's visit had gone well and proved that his bank was invincible. In fact, he thought it had gone so well that he could afford to come the cunt with Teddy as he showed him out through the rather spacious marble foyer where office wankers gathered at lunch time.

'Did you enjoy your time in the vault, Teddy?' asked Chairman Harry with a slick smile.

'Thank you very much, Harry. I've been looking for a safe place for that. It's been in the family for ages. Donkey's years,' enthused Teddy, holding out his hand.

Chairman Harry took it in a firm handshake and the two men locked eyes.

'Well, thank you, Teddy. Thank you for choosing us,' said Harry.

'No, this is perfect for me. I'm well impressed. It feels very safe, very safe indeed,' replied Teddy with a big smile.

Harry smiled back.

'Rest assured, Teddy, we're very safe.' Harry suddenly dropped the smile. 'Very safe indeed. Do we understand each other?'

The two of them still hadn't broken eye contact. Eventually, Teddy said, 'Well, that's very comforting to know. Harry, it's been nice doing business with you. I'll see you around.'

Teddy turned and walked into the revolving doors, which whisked him away and into the street. He stepped back into the carbon-monoxide-stinking real world. Chairman Harry watched him disappear along the crowded pavement and smiled.

Fucker.

Teddy headed away from the black-glassed building of Imperial Emblatt, past a dry cleaner's, past a Turkish baths, past the golden arches of McDonald's, past a Lloyd's Bank and then casually wove his way in between the flow of vehicles towards his parked Jaguar.

As Teddy opened the passenger door, Stan, sitting in the driver's seat, started the engine. Teddy had a strange kind of half-smile on his face.

He looks like he wants to fuck Harry right up the arse.

'And?' prompted Stan.

'And what?' said Teddy, still smiling to himself.

Stan pulled away from the kerb and eased the car into the busy London traffic.

'What do you reckon, then? Is the job possible? Is it impossible? Yes? No? How'd it look? Too big? Too flash? Are we on or not?' demanded Stan.

'I'll tell you what, Stan, that place is fucking impressive. That vault is the vault of the Starship fucking Enterprise. Harry's got it sewn up brilliant!' enthused Teddy.

Stan put his foot down and dodged through a yellow light.

'Yeah? But is it do-able?' Stan wanted to know.

'I don't see why not,' said Teddy, turning and giving Stan a broad smile. 'Where there's a will – and there is a fucking will – there's a way. And there is a fucking way.'

From the moment that Teddy Bass had seen inside Harry's vault he was like a cat trying to get at a canary. He had to have it.

Teddy's first idea involved the kidnapping of close and dearly beloved family members of the night-time security staff, threatening the safety of their various bodily parts until the guards agreed to help with Teddy's little plan. While this was a bright idea and perfectly workable on paper, it had one unavoidable flaw. There were no security guards. None. In the daytime, the building was crawling with people, but at night, the system was fully automatic. It relied on fifty million pounds' worth of computer surveillance equipment and the safest fuck-off underground vault in Europe. Maybe someone high up in some office somewhere had been smart enough to work out that security guards might even turn out to be a liability.

Teddy's next idea was the sewers – but the public plans showed that this too was a nonstarter. The nearest sewer was more than a hundred feet away to the south and it would require about six months of twenty-four-hour nonstop drilling to even reach the fucking vault.

After three and a half weeks of no progress what-so-fucking-ever, Teddy had Stan take pictures of the Imperial Emblatt building. The pictures covered every conceivable angle: the black glass front with its giant revolving doors, the side alley used by smokers for a quick fag while skiving from their desks, and the building's rear with its rusting fire escapes and huge industrial dustbins which stank even when empty.

It got Teddy nowhere.

Neither did an idea about the large air-conditioning units on the roof. They could be opened, no worries, but they didn't lead into the vault, which had an entirely different air pumping system hidden deep underground.

Stan suggested the idea of releasing a deadly computer virus into the building security computer to screw it up and allow them access. It was potentially a fantastic and forward-thinking idea – but since neither he nor Teddy knew their arse from their Internet, and since it didn't exactly seem the sort of thing you could ask about over the counter at Dixon's, it too died a death.

Teddy spent long evenings standing on his penthouse balcony staring out over the cityscape, with just a crystal tumbler of whisky for company. Finally, he was drawn back to the building himself. Across the street at the day's end, he would watch the revolving doors spit out the steady stream of baggy-eyed nine-to-fivers desperate for home.

On the third day, Teddy stayed until the building was

darkened and empty. The figure of Harry emerged from the doors – like a good little Chairman he'd stayed late at the office. A shiny black car and driver were waiting to whisk Chairman Harry away, but dismissing them was the work of a moment and he walked off along the pavement.

On impulse, Teddy decided to follow Chairman Harry on his night-time wanderings. He didn't have to go far. Chairman Harry turned the corner and walked straight into the Turkish baths.

Teddy followed him into the foyer and loitered out of sight, pretending to make a call on the public phone secreted in the corner. From the receptionist's reaction, Chairman Harry was obviously a regular and he disappeared down a flight of stairs into the steamy interior of the building.

Teddy approached the reception but, before he had decided what to say, the young man at the desk sized him up quickly as an embarrassed newcomer. He handed over a set of towels and took a ten pound note without offering any change.

Loud male voices boomed through the white clouds of steam and echoed off the tiled walls which were yellowing with age. Teddy found an empty cubicle – the old-fashioned kind that he remembered from school swimming trips – and soon emerged wrapped in the middle-sized white towel that he'd been given.

The steam carried the heavy stench of chlorine into Teddy's nostrils. Fat men sat on benches, trying hard to sweat away their business account lunches. Teddy walked past them and headed down towards the main pool room. Wandering casually inside, his eyes darted around, looking for Chairman Harry.

Teddy sat on a hard wooden bench at the side of the pool

and, with a half-smile on his face, he watched the fat, naked bodies of middle-aged men bob in and out of the water. He realized he felt horribly out of place, a completely unwelcome intruder into their strange water-baby games. Teddy suddenly wondered what he was doing there, in these deep and dank underground baths.

Then, on the other side of the pool, he saw Chairman Harry limbering up, readying himself to dive. Voices from the water were raised in encouragement as Harry dropped his towel to the tiled floor and dived ungracefully, his stomach swaying, into the murky depths.

As Teddy watched him hit the water, he realized that he suddenly knew exactly what to do. As Chairman Harry's flabby thighs pushed him deeper into the grubby pool, Teddy realized that it could work. Finally, as Chairman Harry's fingers touched the cracked and broken tiles at the bottom, Teddy couldn't help but smile with relief.

The plan was perfect.

By the time that Chairman Harry's head appeared above the surface of the water a few seconds later, Teddy Bass was long gone. He had a job to pull off, and now he knew exactly how he was going to do it . . .

11. 'Do the job'

Don had finally finished explaining the convoluted history of the job to Gal and stood, looking very pleased with himself, on Gal's Spanish patio. It was a story that Teddy had told Stan, that Stan had passed on to Don, and now Don had relayed to Gal, the last link in the growing chain.

Gal watched Don cowering under the noon sun, his eyes reduced to slits. Gal had done nine years because of him. Nine whole years of his life wasted sitting in a dark, dank hole. Nine years wearing a grey uniform rotting in a grey room. Nine years inside.

'So they ask me to put a team together and I'm only gonna say yes, aren't I? One – because I'm like that. Two – because it's a diamond of a job. Every way you look at it, it's fucking perfect. Three – because it gave me a right hard-on just thinking about it!' grinned Don. 'You see, Gal, like Teddy says, where there's a will – and there is a fucking will – there's a way. And there is a fucking way. There's always a fucking way ...'

'Yeah, and there's always a fucking way to get caught as well!' Gal couldn't help interjecting. 'Anything can go wrong, even with the best plan. Anything can happen – I'm living testament to that, ain't I?'

Don wasn't pleased.

'Oh, turn the record over, for fuck's sake. Gal, wake up, will you? This is Teddy! Teddy Bass we're talking about. Mr Black Magic, Mr Einstein a-go-go. He's an absolute beast, mate,' enthused Don. 'You don't know the way his mind works! This job is beautiful! It's a work of art. They'll bring back hanging for this one! It's a fucking insult, Gal.'

Gal remained less than impressed.

'We're gonna cream their arses with a golden dildo and be gone by the time they wake up sore! Red faces all round, read all about it!' continued Don. 'We'll make the main evening news, my son, and I don't mean the fucking cuddly animal story at the end.' It was obvious – Don wasn't likely to take 'No' for an answer.

Gal said nothing.

'Unbelievable! Un-fucking-believeable!' declared Don. 'Anybody else would be queuing round the block to get a sniff of this. Anyway, we're looking at moving in on Saturday, but you'll be needed in London to meet the rest of the fellas and prepare on Friday, all right? The briefing's at The Bungalow, nine o'clock Saturday night. We'll take you through it. Piece of piss, really. Check in Friday, check out Sunday, all right?'

Oh God. Friday? This Friday? So soon. Have to tell him no. Tell him now.

'Bit sudden, isn't it?' said Gal, trying to hide his alarm.

'Sudden? Fuck, no. It's very far from sudden! Teddy's been working on this nearly full-time for five months. Stan's been on it nearly as long, and I've been in on it for two! Preparation. Preparation. Preparation. 'Snot sudden. It's just that you are the very last piece in the jigsaw. As far as the actual job's concerned, a monkey with no bollocks could do it! That's why I thought of you!' smiled Don.

73

'Cheers, Don,' said Gal.

If you wanna insult me, stop asking me to do the bloody job.

'It's all set up. The rest of the lads are ready. I've booked hotel rooms round town for the visitors like you. Different hotels, all paid for by cash, untraceable, of course. You're at the Grosvenor. You're booked in as Mr Rowntree – like Smarties – like Shaft,' Don informed him. 'If anyone gives you a pull, say you're just back to see some friends. Havin' a social visit to see family, right? Someone'll call you Friday morning. Pick you up. Probably Mike, if he's finished the loading by then. OK?'

Go on, tell him no.

Don watched carefully as Gal's head nodded in a faint and noncommittal way.

'What's that supposed to mean?' he asked with a sneer.

'What?' said Gal, absent-mindedly. He wasn't even aware of what he'd been doing.

'That stupid nodding you're doing? What does that mean? Is that a yes?' demanded Don, aggression growing in his voice.

Gal found that his eyes were suddenly frozen, staring at the ground between his feet. Don moved nearer and tried to catch Gal's vision, but Gal couldn't bring himself to look directly back. Don was hovering like a cobra ready to spit venom.

'Is this a fuck-off, Gal?' said Don, directly.

Tell him. Tell him. Tell him.

''Course not, Don.'

'Are you saying no?'

'No,' said Gal, trying to appease.

'Is that what you're saying?' said Don, coming closer to Gal.

74

'No, not exactly ...' said Gal.

'Then, what exactly *are* you saying?' Don asked, a touch of impatience creeping into his voice.

Gal had to choose his words very carefully.

Explain it to him. Tell him why not.

'What I'm saying is ... thanks, and all that. Thanks for thinking of me, and asking me and that, but I'm just gonna have to turn the opportunity down ...' Gal tried, tentatively.

Shit.

'No, you're just gonna have to change your mind and turn this opportunity into a yes!' said Don, fast and angry.

'I can't, Don,' pleaded Gal.

Shit. He's losing it.

'Can, cunt, can! Can, you cunt, can! Cunt! "Can't"! You cunt!' exploded Don, his face leering at Gal with extreme hatred.

Gal averted his eyes from Don's and caught sight of his own ever-expanding waistline. The growing mound of blubber around his middle was the result of too many days drinking beer in the sun, too many fine meals in restaurants, and too little to worry about.

Tell him you're too fat.

'I'm not exactly match fit,' said Gal, patting his stomach, sending waves bouncing through the expansive flesh.

'You seem all right to me!'

'Well, not really, Don. The exercise thing's gone a bit to pot. I don't run any more, or do weights. Don't even swim, really,' said Gal.

Convince him you'd be useless.

'You look great – you're fine!'

'No, I'm really not. I'd let you down, Don,' said Gal.

'Do the job,' Don cut in sharply.

Leave me alone.

'What?' Gal was almost stunned by the directness of the request. 'No, Don. I can't.'

'Yes.'

'No.'

'Yes.'

'I can't.'

'You can!'

'I can't!'

'Fat cunt!'

'Don't do this, Don,' said Gal. He had the feeling that he was being slowly tortured to death.

'Do what?'

'Look . . .' began Gal, but Don was close to boiling point.

'*What* am I doing? I'm trying to make you some money. I'm trying to do you a huge fucking favour. I'm trying to help you out, so you tell me, *what* am I doing?' he shouted.

'This . . . all this. This,' said Gal, his arms gesturing around him.

Stop fucking picking me to pieces.

'This? This what?' Don played dumb.

'Oh Don, come *on* . . .'

Somewhere in the demented workings of Don's head something clicked and decided on a change of tactics.

'All right, we'll drop it. It's dropped,' he announced quietly, stepping back away from Gal. Then he added, modestly alarmed, 'There's a boy over there – gawping at us.'

'What?'

Gal looked round and saw that Enrique was standing just behind the garden wall watching them. His young face was a mask of concern and worry.

76

Get him out of here. Get him out now.

Gal thought quickly. 'Enrique, you go home, son. I don't need you today. You go home.'

Enrique didn't move.

'He's staring at me,' said Don, low and quiet.

Out of Don's eyeline, Gal gave Enrique an expression which said, 'For Christ's sake, fuck off *now*.'

'This is Don – Don Logan. He's a friend of mine from England come over for a visit,' explained Gal. 'We've got to talk about something now, so you get yourself off home. Go on.'

Finally, still keeping his suspicious eyes firmly fixed on Don, Enrique reluctantly started to leave.

'Who was that little cunt?' asked Don.

'Local boy, lives with his mother further up the valley. His dad did a runner – usual story. He helps me around the house with bits and bobs. Knows everyone round here. Nice kid, actually.'

'If you say so,' said Don, unconvinced.

'Do you wanna go into town and have a drink, Don? I'll show you round the place if you like,' said Gal, changing the subject entirely.

'If you like, I'm not fussed,' came the enthusiastic reply.

Gal walked towards the house trying to remember where his car keys were.

'You're on two per cent, two-and-a-half, maybe even three – depends on the usual bumflufferies,' Don told him.

What the fuck ... ?

Gal stopped in the doorway.

'But it's not about the money with me and you, Gal, is it? It's the charge. It's the bolt. It's the buzz. It's the sheer fuck-off-ness of it all! Am I right? It's Fernando Rey on a tube

77

train giving the finger to Gene Hackman! Am I wrong?' gushed Don.

Gal suddenly found himself warming to Don's school-kid enthusiasm.

'Well, actually, Don, I gotta say that it was always about the money for me,' said Gal, wryly.

'That's what prostitutes say ...' observed Don.

'Do they? Ah well ...'

'You saying you're a prostitute?' asked Don, keenly.

'Well, everyone is to a certain extent, aren't they?' reasoned Gal.

'What – a prossie? A whore?'

'You gotta get your money to survive somehow,' said Gal, stepping into the kitchen and searching the worktop for his keys.

'That's prostitution!' called Don's voice.

'Call it what you will, mate,' shouted back Gal.

'You're not a prostitute, Gal ... So who's the prostitute then? You saying it's me?' said Don, aggression returning to his voice once more.

Gal came out of the house with his car keys in his hand and saw Don standing staring at him ready for another confrontation.

Christ.

'Do you wanna fuck me, Gal?'

Would he ever stop?

'Fuck off, Don.'

Gal walked towards his car waiting in the driveway. He heard Don's footsteps following behind.

Utter bastard.

'Is that what you want? You couldn't afford me anyway! Beside, you're the cunt with tits. Look at you! You should

78

have a bra to keep those two under control! You're giving me a hard-on just looking!' said Don, his mood lifting with every abusive insult that he got off his chest and on to Gal's.

'Yeah, all right, Don,' sighed Gal, gently. 'No need to get personal.'

Don smiled to himself. There was plenty of need to get personal, and Don hadn't started yet. This was just the warm-up.

12. 'What d'you make of a woman
who'd want to do that?'

Gal decided not to take Don to any of his regular bars in case he got irritated and killed someone.

Don seemed to take the car journey as some kind of break between boxing rounds and sat in silence for most of the way. In the middle of a long stretch of deserted highway, Don wound down the window and leaned his head out, staring at the distant hills. It reminded Gal of having a dog in the car.

Gal parked outside his least favourite bar in town and they went into the noisy interior which was full of locals, drinking and arguing. Gal bought the beers and they stood at the bar to drink them.

'We come into town a few times a week, and every now and then Deedee drives into the city,' Gal told Don, trying to keep up the pretence of normality. 'It's less than an hour from here.'

Don was staring at a woman dancing with her boyfriend on the other side of the room.

'She's all right that Jackie, isn't she?' said Don, out of the blue.

'Yeah, she's great. A laugh,' agreed Gal.

'Big tits,' said Don.

Gal looked uncomfortable. 'Yeah, like I said, she's a lovely girl.'

'Listen, Gal, I've missed my plane by now. Never get out to the airport in time from this bloody place. Is it all right with you if I stay the night?' asked Don.

Of course you've missed your bloody plane. You missed it hours ago, you shit. You were never going to get it. You were never going back today, you bastard.

'Yeah, 'course it is, Don. We'd love to have you,' lied Gal.

'I fucked her,' announced Don.

'Who?'

'Jackie, of course. I had her,' repeated Don, rather proudly.

Fucking hell.

This was news to Gal. Entirely shocking and unpleasant news – that the partner of his best friend and a close friend herself had fucked this raving bastard monster. And the way Don had just said it, Gal knew it had to be true.

'That's really not my business, Don.'

'Yeah, I know. I'm just telling you, ain't I?' Don explained. 'Three years ago it was. Remember that time when she came over to see her mum? It was then. She got in touch with Toni and we all went out down the Curry Garden, you know. She's a right dirty cow. Filthy. She loves it! Can't get enough of it!'

Gal was rather at a loss for words.

'Yeah?'

'Aitch knows fuck-all about it, of course. What's she doing wasting her time with that lanky hunk of piss anyway?

He's a fucking pillock!' said Don, pressing his beer bottle against his forehead in an attempt to cool himself down.

'He loves her, Don.'

'I'm tempted to tell him,' said Don, looking at Gal to gauge his reaction. 'I know what he likes! I'm telling you, if he looks at me the wrong way, I'm gonna fucking kill him, you see if I don't.'

Then Don moved nearer and in confidential, hushed tones said, 'During what we were doing, she tried to stick her finger up my bum! I almost hit the roof, you can imagine. What do you make of that, Gal? What d'you make of a woman who'd want to do that?'

'Nothing wrong with that,' said Gal, struggling to get the unsavoury image of the bizarre coupling of Don and Jackie out of his mind.

What the fuck was she thinking of?

Don seemed to take stock of Gal's comment, then with obvious difficulty said, 'Listen, don't say nothing, Gal. Keep this to yourself, all right? But I, er ... I quite liked her ...' he admitted, the confession squeezing itself out of him like a constipated turd.

'Did you?' said Gal, simply.

'How is she? Is she all right?' said Don, too quickly.

Gal had had enough. 'What's that, Don? Didn't quite catch it.'

'You 'eard!'

'No, I didn't, Don, sorry.' Gal shook his head, sounding quite genuine.

'Yeah, well, I'm not repeatin' it,' said Don. 'How far's the sea, then?'

Night. Enrique ran along the sand keeping his back arched

and his head low. He kept his eyes fixed firmly on two figures further down the beach in the distance. When one of the figures looked round, taking in the view, Enrique threw himself on to a sand dune and instantly disappeared from sight.

The sand was soft and fine and still felt warm with the afterglow of the day's heat. Enrique could smell the sea salt from the breaking ocean waves and, just in front of him, rotting seaweed lay strewn across the top of the dune, left there by the day's high tide.

Enrique had abandoned his moped, leaving it hidden between two tall sand dunes further back. He had found the two Englishmen surprisingly easy to follow. They seemed so intent on watching each other's every move that the rest of the world around them was nothing but an unwelcome distraction to be ignored.

After he had deliberately let himself be spotted at Gal's villa – just to let Gal know that he was around – Enrique had hardly let the two men out of his sight.

Of course, he'd lost them temporarily as Gal's vehicle had out-paced his moped into the town, but it had been easy enough to locate the parked car. First Enrique had tried a couple of Gal's favourite haunts, then, thinking about what he'd already observed, he'd headed straight for the bar where Gal never went. That was where he'd found Gal's car.

The fact that Gal was avoiding his regular night spots only alarmed Enrique more, and when he saw Gal and Don finally leaving he made sure that he didn't lose them again. He didn't like the look of Don Logan one bit. Why had he come so far from England to cause trouble for his part-time boss? Why had Mrs Gal and the others so obviously left Gal to deal with him alone? Whatever the reason, Gal *wasn't* alone. Enrique was there – following and watching to make sure nothing bad happened.

He had followed them to the beach, via another bar, and was now trailing them along the shoreline. Unlikely as it sounded, Gal and Don seemed to be enjoying what would otherwise have been a romantic moonlit walk. Enrique kept close to the ground, wriggling close enough to eavesdrop on their conversation.

Gal and Don were standing on the beach looking out at the dark rolling sea, which was almost black under the clear night sky.

'Big, innit?' observed Don, aimlessly.

''S beautiful ...'

'Did you know that two-thirds of the world is the sea, did ya know that?' said Don. 'They reckon that it's the last great unexplored place on earth and all that, don't they?'

'Is that right?'

''Cause there's so much sea and oceans – that's why the earth looks blue from the moon,' added Don.

'Yeah, I know. And they reckon that the only man-made thing you can see from up there is the Great Wall of China ...' Gal told him, not to be outdone.

Don took a moment to think.

'Not sure about that . ... Not Westminster Abbey or St Paul's Cathedral, then? I should think you could see Big bloody Ben from the moon. I mean, with a telescope or something to help you ...' suggested Don.

Gal decided not to argue. 'Maybe ...'

Silence.

Gal could feel Don's eyes watching him closely. Searching for that chink in his armour to stab through.

'You can talk to me, Gal. I'm here for you, I'm a good

listener,' coaxed Don, in the style of a radio agony aunt probing a confession of sexual deviance from a nun.

He's giving you a chance. Take it.

'Well, what can I say, Don? I've said it all. It's a great offer, and thanks and that, but I'm retired,' said Gal softly, as another wave crashed over the sand in front of them.

'Shut up!' snapped Don.

He didn't want to hear this.

'There it is. It's no use, Don,' said Gal.

'Shut your fucking mouth!' exploded Don, suddenly angry again and full of hate. He balled his fist and waved it in Gal's general direction.

'Do you want me to belt you? Cunt! You louse! You've got some fucking nerve, Gal Dove! Ain't ya?' Don yelled. 'Retired? Do fuck off! And when you've fucked off come back and fuck off again. You're revolting! Look at you. Fucking barbecue suntan!' He paused, following his own instruction.

'You look like you're made out of fucking leather. I could make a suitcase out of your fucking skin! I bet I'd get two nice holdalls out of your arse. You're like a crocodile. A fat bastard crocodile,' he continued. 'You're fucking Idi Amin, my son. D'you know what I mean? Jesus, the state of you. You oughta be ashamed. Who d'you think you are? King of the castle? Cock of the walk?'

Don moved quickly and, before Gal could stop him, he kneed Gal in the side of the thigh. Gal winced in pain and felt the numbness of a dead-leg begin to spread. He let himself fall on to the inviting sand.

Hidden among the nearby dunes, Enrique strained to see what was happening. He was ready to shout or run for help if he decided Gal needed it.

Don paced around in front of Gal, his anger growing.

'What do you think this is? The Wheel of Fortune? You think you can just make your dough and then fuck off? Leave the table? Thanks, Don. See ya, Don, I'm off to sunny Spain now, Don, so long and thanks for all the fish. Fuck off, Don,' the bald bastard ranted on.

'It's not like that, Don,' said Gal, in barely more than a whisper.

'Isn't it? It fucking feels like it is. You lie in your waterless swimming pool like a fat, flabby blob laughing at me! Do you think I'm going to have that? Do you *really* think I'm going to have that happen? You ponce. Do you hate me that much? You cunt!'

'I don't hate you, Don,' insisted Gal.

'You fucking hate me, all right. You must hate me to treat me like this,' said Don, throwing his arms wide to show just how abused he felt.

'I don't.'

Don locked eyes with Gal again and leaned down towards where Gal lay in the sand.

'*Why* do you hate me so much? Tell your Uncle Don why you hate him all of a sudden and why you think that he's such a cunt.'

'Please, Don,' begged Gal.

'Say it. Say, "I hate you, Don."'

Gal struggled up from the sand and began brushing grains from his trousers. 'I'm not saying that!' he replied, firmly.

'All right then. If you haven't got the guts to say it, I'll say it for you. "I – hate – you – Don." There!' gloated Don.

'I've had enough of this,' said Gal, turning and beginning to walk back up the beach and away from his tormentor.

Without warning, Don attacked Gal from behind. Mov-

86

ing quickly, Don delivered two fast but powerful punches. While Gal was still off-balance, Don grabbed Gal's hair, spun him round and threw him back down on to the sand.

As Gal disappeared from sight once more, Enrique slid nearer across the sands, trying to ascertain the seriousness of the situation.

Don was now standing over Gal, his looming figure casting a shadow across Gal's body in the bright moonlight.

'Do the job! *Do* the job! Do the fucking job! You're doing it! You're fucking well doing it, because I say you're fucking well doing it! Look at you. Where's your fucking dignity, eh?'

'What do you want me to say, Don?' asked Gal, cowering from another possible onslaught from the bald man's relentless fists.

'Don't get all intellectual with me – it doesn't suit you. And don't try and take the piss either – I don't like it. Well?' demanded Don.

'Don ...'

'Listen to yourself. You're pathetic. All right, all right. I'll make it easy for you – God, you're fucking trying at times!' Don raised his eyes heavenwards before resuming his pacing across the sand. 'Are you gonna do the job? It's not a difficult question – yes or no?'

'No.'

'*Yes*! Fuck off! Wanker. You're *doing* it!' bellowed Don.

For a few seconds, Don stood with his fists ready to strike, then, without another word he walked away from Gal towards where they had left the car. From his hiding place, Enrique watched the man retreating with great relief. He wanted to let Gal know that he had been watching him, ready to protect him – but he knew that would have to wait.

Gal picked himself up again, once more brushed the

grains of fine sand from his shirt and trousers, and limped after Don.

When Gal reached the car, Don was already sitting inside like a man impatient for his driver to return to work.

'Shall we head back to the house then, Don?' suggested Gal, starting the engine, 'The others should be back by now. Bound to be, ain't they?'

Silence.

Gal put the car into gear and performed a perfect three-point turn. He sped off down the beach road, the rear wheels of the car spraying a light cloud of sand in their wake. The roar of Gal's engine hid another quieter noise behind them. It was the sound of a second-hand moped being carefully coaxed into life by its young owner.

13. 'The steak was like that'

As they drove back to the villa, Gal imagined the horror that Deedee would feel when he returned to their home with Don Logan still in tow. He imagined that the others would have returned late afternoon to find the house empty. Perhaps they would even think that he was doing the return airport run for Don. Dropping him at Gate 14, waving him off, and then returning . . . alone. The thought of Don leaving the country, leaving them to get on with their lives, seemed to be the only thing that he wanted in the whole world.

Fuck off, Don. Just fuck off home.

Don would go, Gal's swimming pool would be repaired and everything would be perfect once again. Everything would be back like it was before Don arrived to fuck it all up.

Don's silence during the drive suited Gal but unfortunately, like all good things, it had to come to an end. Don stopped staring out of the window at the nothingness around them and cleared his throat, gobbing the resulting ball of spit out of the car window, which luckily happened to be open.

'Do you know what I've noticed, Gal?' asked Don.

Gal hoped Don was about to highlight an interesting piece of trivia about night in Spain, but the knot of tension in his stomach suspected otherwise.

'Do you know what stands out crystal clear? In all the time since I got here this morning, you haven't once asked about anybody back home – and that saddens me. That really sticks in my throat,' hissed Don.

'I haven't had the chance, we've been—'

Don interrupted.

'Everyone's always asking after you. *How's* Gal? *What's* he doing? Is he all right? Have you heard from him lately? It's embarrassing. I always have to say, "No, not for a while." It leaves me wondering if I've done something to upset you. *Have* I done something to upset you, Gal?' asked Don, directly.

'Of course you haven't.'

'Meaning what, exactly?'

'Meaning that of course you haven't,' repeated Gal.

'Where were you born?' said Don, suddenly.

'Er … Ilford Maternity Hospital, just off the Romford Road, but what's …?'

'You were born in Britain!' shouted Don. 'You're not a fucking Dago, layabout Spaniard. Don't kid yourself. You're making yourself into a laughing stock out here!'

Don suddenly lurched forward as Gal violently slammed on the brakes, his hands instinctively slapping on to the dashboard to stop him from banging his head.

'Jesus!'

As Don struggled to regain his composure, he caught sight of something moving through the windscreen. In the middle of the road, caught squarely in the car's headlights, was a small horned animal.

'What's that?'

'It's a goat,' explained Gal, opening his car door. 'They're a fucking nuisance out here.'

Gal pushed himself out of the car, while Don regarded the goat with considerable horror.

'He's staring at me. What's he staring at me for?' called Don.

'He's not staring at you. He's just looking at the car lights,' Gal tried to reassure him.

'He's fucking staring at me!' insisted Don, also climbing out of the car and nervously following Gal towards the paralyzed creature.

Don edged closer as if working his way through a minefield. 'It won't charge, will it?' he asked, getting ready to jump if it did.

'Don, he's a Spanish goat, not a fucking African rhinoceros,' said Gal. 'He's not going to charge at anything.'

Gal waved his arms in the goat's general direction and the animal turned and trotted off into the desert. The two men got back inside the car.

'He was definitely,' said Don, 'looking at me funny.'

Aitch was doing what he did best. He was lying.

'Cor, the steak was like that!' he grinned, indicating a size of about eighteen inches across with his hands. 'The bloody size of the thing. I couldn't finish it! Very nice place. We'll take you there some time, Gal. Staff was nice too, weren't they? Our waiter was very attentive. Handsome fucker as well. Bloody Adonis. He liked you well enough, didn't he, Deedee? He liked you all right.'

Gal, Aitch, Deedee, Jackie and Don were sitting around the low table in Gal's lounge. Obviously the other three had been delighted to see that Gal had returned with Don and were overjoyed that he was staying the night so that they could all enjoy his company for a few precious hours longer. The lovely Jackie looked particularly pleased by this development. So pleased, that she looked like she might be inclined to slit her wrists at any moment.

In fact, Deedee had already worked out that Don Logan was likely to be inflicting himself upon them for at least another day before Gal actually arrived back with him. When she had returned to the house with Aitch and Jackie, the first thing she had done was to check the spare room upstairs. There, despite her best hopes, were Don's bag, clothes and his passport.

Bastard.

'Yeah, he liked you all right,' repeated Aitch, desperate to maintain some kind of light conversation around the table and keep the increasingly awkward silence at bay.

'Well, he's got good taste then,' said Gal, forcing a smile.

'And it wasn't very expensive neither,' added Aitch.

Gal flashed his eyes at Aitch to say that perhaps it was time to stop talking about the nonexistent restaurant before Don inevitably decided he wanted to have a nonexistent meal there.

'You sound very nice on the phone, Jackie,' said Don suddenly, and without any relevance to the rest of the conversation. 'You've got a nice telephone voice. You sound like you work in an office! Have you ever worked in an office?'

This was hugely unwelcome attention for Jackie.

'No,' she said, without raising her eyes from the floor.

'No? Shame. It's a nice telephone voice, very nice,' said Don.

The awkward silence descended once again.

'I've worked in an office. I worked in an office one summer when I was seventeen. Does that surprise you?' offered Don to the room in general.

'What, that you were seventeen?' cut in Deedee, her voice cold with disdain, suddenly tired of the whole pretence of niceness.

Don stared across at her, surprised by her abrupt hostility. Aitch looked at Gal with fear in his eyes.

'You've got nice eyes, Deedee. Never noticed them before. Are they real?' said Don with a tiny smile.

For him this was high wit.

Gal stood up. 'I'll get us all another drink,' he said, heading to the kitchen.

'I'll give you a hand,' said Deedee, following him.

Gal had been in Don's company for the best part of twelve hours and it was a relief just to be in another room from him.

'He's staying the night. There nothing I could do about it. He missed his plane out today,' explained Gal.

'Did you tell him?' whispered Deedee, as Gal opened the fridge door.

'Of course I've told him. He's only asked me about a million times so far, and each time I've told him that I'm retired. I'm not interested. OK?'

'So why's he still here?' Deedee demanded.

'Because, sadly, it's not that simple. Because, sadly, the cunt won't take no for an answer, that's why.'

Gal handed Deedee two beer bottles. 'And why didn't you tell me about him and Jackie?' he added in a hiss.

'What about him and ... oh.' Deedee stopped, suddenly realizing what Gal was talking about. 'Because she asked me not to.'

'Oh, she asked you not to. That's great – nice one,'

huffed Gal. 'Well, that could've been very important information. I mean I might have played things different if I had
known.'

Gal and Deedee stared at each other coldly.

'Sorry, love.'

'As it was, he gets to tell me while we're casually chatting
at a bar. Just drops it into the conversation, like, and I have
to avoid choking on my beer. What the fuck was she *playing*
at?!' Gal demanded.

Before Deedee could answer, the kitchen door swung
open and Aitch walked in.

'This is a fucking nightmare,' he said, understating the
obvious. 'The man's a fucking nightmare. What happened
when you were gone? What did he say? Have you told
him yet?'

'Yeah, I've told him I'm retired and he's told me he won't
take no for an answer. And he's staying the night because he
missed his plane,' explained Gal yet again.

Next door in the lounge, Jackie and Don Logan were left
awkwardly alone.

When he didn't think that she was looking, Don stole a
quick glance along Jackie's legs. He was about to do it again,
when she suddenly got up and, without a word, went into
the kitchen. She joined the others standing by the open
fridge, enjoying the feel of the cool air cascading out.

'Have you told him yet?' she asked Gal, who had had
enough of that particular question.

'Yes, I told him that I'm retired, and he won't give up,
and he's missed his plane, and he's staying the night, all
fucking right? Everybody clear now?'

'This is a fucking nightmare,' said Jackie, wondering why
the other three were suddenly looking at her like she'd put

her foot in it. 'Well, it *is*!'

'Yes, we know it is,' hissed Gal.

Gal noticed that Aitch was leaning over the sink, straining his neck to see out of the window.

'He's gone outside. What's he doing now?' said Aitch.

Gal looked for himself.

Don was by the patio wall. He seemed to be leaning down carefully looking for something on the surface of the stonework. He moved forward and gingerly eased aside the branches of a bush with his toe.

'I bet he's looking for that lizard we saw this afternoon,' remembered Gal.

'Lizard?'

'Come on, we'd better all get out there. This is looking a bit bleeding obvious,' said Gal, ordering his very reluctant troops back on to the battlefield. 'He must be tired – maybe he'll want to go to bed soon,' he added, trying to convince himself as much as them.

'I hope you're bleeding right,' said Aitch.

This was going to be a very long night indeed.

14. House guest

Eventually it was Gal and Deedee who had to suggest bed. Aitch and Jackie had departed to the relative sanctuary of their own home leaving Mr and Mrs Dove alone with their house guest.

Despite half a dozen attempts by Don to get Gal talking about the good old days, Gal had managed to persuade him that they all needed some sleep. (Gal had obviously steered well clear of suggesting that they should all 'retire' for the night for fear of word-associating Don into another violent rage.)

Gal and Deedee's bedroom door had no lock on it for the simple reason that they had never ever needed one. It was one of the oversights that came from not entertaining psychopaths on a regular basis. Neither Gal nor Deedee felt like talking as they slipped under the covers. Both of them, especially Gal, were utterly exhausted. Both of them also had trouble sleeping. They were used to having the house entirely to themselves, except when Aitch and Jackie stayed over after a big drinking session. Don staying down the hallway was like having a poisonous snake loose in the house.

About an hour after going to bed, Gal and Deedee were still desperately trying to get to sleep when their bedroom door began to inch its way open very slowly. Neither of them moved a muscle, but their eyes flickered quickly open.

Don Logan stared in through the gap, watching them as they lay in bed. For a few seconds, they could hear his shallow breathing, then the door slowly inched shut again and Don's footsteps disappeared down the hallway. Underneath the covers, Gal's hand found Deedee's and squeezed it tightly.

Don closed the bathroom door behind him and noticed that it had no lock. He crossed to the toilet, unzipped his trousers and began to take a leak. Halfway through, Don casually twisted his hips and aimed at the floor, deliberately creating a yellow stain in the carpet. The smell of warm piss rose pungently in the cool night air.

He moved over and stared at his reflection in the large mirror above the sink. He stared at himself as if he was squaring up for a fight. Then he leaned closer and whispered to his reflection in an urgent, confidential tone:

'What you playing at? You shouldn't have told him that. You shouldn't have said anything there. Where? There in that bar. Should have kept your mouth shut about Jackie. Jackie the Paki. What, Gal? No, he's all right, but you're still giving too much of yourself away, mate! Watch your fucking mouth. Best keep schtum, old son.'

Don looked around the bathroom to see if any of the inanimate objects in there with him were eavesdropping on his conversation with himself. They didn't seem to be.

'Big mouth. Big fucking mouth, Don! Ah, don't worry about it. He won't say nothing. Nothing to say, is there? What does he know? It's not a bad thing to say,' decided

Don. Then he changed his mind. Again.

'Staple your lips to your gums, you cunt! You sappy little cunt!' Don told his reflection, in a suddenly lower and more sinister tone of voice. 'Now from Norwich, it's the quiz of the week. From porridge. Shut your mouth. Please Sir, shut your mouth. That's it. It's shut. Shut it now and don't say another fucking thing.'

Don saw Gal's yellow swimming trucks hanging on the small bathroom radiator. Next to them were two small pieces of red cloth, which he recognized as a bikini. Deedee's bikini. He slowly picked up the top part and put one cup on the top of his head where it perched like an undersized hat. The other cup dangled down over his right ear. Don looked like a small monkey trying to wear human clothes.

He stared at himself in the mirror for several more minutes before he finally put the red top back on the radiator. He left both taps running in the sink, then turned out the bathroom light as he left.

When Gal woke up from a sleep he hadn't realized he'd succumbed to, he could hear the quiet sound of Don's voice somewhere very close by. Gal focused his eyes and saw the shape of Don squatting down beside the bed, staring straight at him. It was the middle of the night, with no sign of dawn.

Deedee lay on the opposite side of the bed; from the sound and rate of her breathing, Gal could tell that she was still asleep.

Thank goodness.

'Look at it this way,' invited Don.

Jesus. Will he ever stop?

'Look at it from how I see it. It's like this. I'm a shop-keeper, I've got a nice little shop on the high street, right? Like

Tesco's, only this is Logan's, see? And do you know what's in my shop? All the shelves in Logan's, and all our fridges and all the racks, everywhere you could look, is piled high with money. Stacks and stacks of twenty and fifty pound notes, yeah? Unbelievable amounts of money just sitting there.'

Lying in bed, Gal was a captive audience for Don's fantasy.

'But your Uncle Don, he's not an ordinary shopkeeper, oh no. I'm a different kind altogether. I've got a big sign in the window saying, "Help yourself – Free Money – Bring a Wheelbarrow".'

Don paused to allow Gal to fully take in this marvellous idea.

'So I'm behind the counter. You can hardly see me for money, of course, and everyone's piling into the shop to get their share. The place is full of happy, beaming faces as the punters race round filling up their wheelbarrows. Business is booming. Some greedy fuckers are even coming back for seconds, know what I mean?' he winked.

Gal lay motionless.

'But what do I care? I tell my staff to bring up some more money from the basement. But, just then, what do I see outside the shop? What do I see which both stuns and amazes me?' Don paused a second, for effect. 'It's you! It's my old pal, Gal, and he's walking past the shop without giving it a second glance. I look at you but I don't see a white stick. I don't see a guide dog. Now, what am I supposed to think? How is that gonna make me feel?'

Gal said nothing. In the bed next to him he heard a change in Deedee's breathing. She was awake, he was sure of it.

'I've got to think that you're a cunt, haven't I? So I

quickly throw off my overall and chase after you and I tap you on the shoulder and I say, "Sorry, mate, but I think you've made a mistake. I'm giving away free money back there." And then you look me right in the eyes, just like you're doing right now, right this minute, and you say to me, "That's all right, Don. I'm retired." *Now* can you see my problem, Gal?'

Don waited for a response.

'Could we talk about this in the morning, Don?'

'Do you see what I'm saying, though?' pressed Don.

Gal nodded weakly.

'In the morning, Don, please ...'

Don seemed satisfied that at last he might be getting somewhere with Gal. He carefully and silently backed towards the open bedroom door.

'Come into my shop, Gal. Come into my shop ...' he beckoned like a second-rate TV hypnotist.

With great care, Don pulled the door shut behind him. As it closed, Gal and Deedee, now very much awake, turned to look at each other.

'Jesus!'

Dawn. The sun crept over the hilltops to illuminate another unspoilt blue sky, as it had nearly every day since Gal and Deedee had arrived in Spain.

After Don had described the unique shopping experience that was 'Logan's' with its stacks of free cash, Gal and Deedee had lain awake in each other's arms for what felt like the rest of the night.

As Gal held Deedee through the first light of the early dawn, his thoughts had returned to the boulder that had nearly killed him and had cracked open his precious swimming pool. He began to wonder if it really had been an accident, or if it might have been the work of the Bastard-Monster-Logan. Could he have caused the boulder to start moving all the way from London? Had his hate-filled mind reached out and sent the massive lump of stone tumbling down the hillside to crush Gal and his wonderful life?

Deedee didn't care what had made the rock move and once again suggested the idea of taking flight from Don. But now that he was sleeping two doors along the hall, it seemed an even less sensible idea than yesterday when at least he had been in another country.

Gal's preferred strategy, such as it was, was to do absolutely nothing. Fuck all. It was a tactic based on the logical premise that sooner or later Don would get bored. Failing that, the job itself was on Saturday, and Don would be needed back in London on Friday – giving Don a maximum time of another forty-eight hours in Spain; time in which to poke sharp sticks up Gal's arse and otherwise get on his tits. Given the way that the last twenty-four hours had been, Gal decided that it would probably be touch and go either way.

As they finally dropped into an uneasy doze once more, Gal and Deedee vaguely heard the sound of running water coming from the bathroom. Next door Don was standing in front of a sink full of steaming hot water. The mirror over the sink had misted up several times already. He dragged his razor over the soapy contours of his face, making a slight rasping noise as the blade cut through his dark stubble.

He wiped the mirror again and caught a clear look at his reflection.

'That thing in the window. How much is it?' wondered Don, to himself, his concentration flicking from one piece of his imagination to another without any warning. 'The dog? No, not that one, the other one. The black and white one. What do you call them again? Dalmatian, ain't it? Yeah, all right then, go on, I'll have it. I'll stick it on the mantelpiece beside the clock. You got a head for it?'

Don brought his razor sweeping down the side of his left cheek and splashed it into the sink.

'What is it then, thirteen amp? Yeah, I saw him the other day, he seemed all right. He's had a haircut – either that or his head's got bigger!'

Don edged the razor around the point of his chin, leaning closer to the mirror.

'Are you all right, mate?'

He stopped moving the razor and stared at his own reflection.

'Don't look at me. Is someone taking the piss out of you? *Are* they? Taking liberties? What, that cunt through there? Is he insulting you? What's he said?'

Don was winding himself up.

'It's all right, mate, you can tell me ... he said that, did he? Just like that? No! What, that lump of shit said that? He expects you to swallow that? What, does he think you're a cunt?'

The bald man threw his razor into the sink in disgust.

'I'll sort him out for you, shall I? It's not a problem. We can't have that! Where the fuck is he anyway? What, still in bed?!'

Don, still soapy-faced, burst out of the bathroom and marched along the corridor towards Gal and Deedee's bedroom.

15. *Escape from the*

Planet of the Pussy-nymphs

Under the circumstances, the noise of their bedroom door being thrown open was enough to wake Gal up in an instant. He was halfway through sitting up in bed when Don's fist smashed into his face. Gal felt a familiar numbness spreading along the side of his jaw.

Fuck.

'Get up, you cunt!' bellowed Don, as if he were the victim of some almost unimaginable humiliation. 'It's eight o'clock! You lazy bastard!'

Deedee looked at Don with utter horror and outrage. How dare he barge in here? She saw Gal holding his face, still stunned by the unexpected and unwarranted attack.

'Stop it! Get out of our room!' shrieked Deedee at the top of her voice.

Don stood still, staring down at the startled Gal, who was getting ready to defend himself against further blows if they came. Don slowly turned his head to face Deedee.

She leaned over her husband and cradled him like a lioness.

'Get out, Don,' she ordered, with nothing but hatred and contempt in her voice.

Don paused for a moment, wondering what to do. He had to admit to himself, when he thought about it later, that there was something about her which was ... well, quite scary really.

Don flared his nostrils, then he sniffed and turned back to Gal.

'I'll be downstairs,' he told them, as if that explained everything, and he marched back to the bathroom.

Deedee stayed upstairs out of the way, opting for only a cup of tea for company, while Gal, still in his dressing gown and looking very tired, cooked breakfast – a huge fry-up – for himself and Don.

Two enormous frying pans sizzled on the stove, crammed with four eggs (sunny side up), eight rashers of bacon and seven sausages (all that was left from the barbecue two nights earlier). A saucepan full of baked beans simmered at the back of the stove. A giant American toaster with gleaming silver sides popped up eight slices of hot toast ready for buttering. Gal found space in one of the frying pans to quickly slip in a couple more slices – he felt that in such extreme circumstances, his stress levels deserved the sin of real fried bread.

For the final (and most important) ingredient, Gal reached down and opened the cupboard next to the cooker. Sitting on the floor at the bottom was an industrial-sized catering pack of the largest bottles of HP Sauce that could be legally obtained. Gal took out a new bottle, twisted off the shiny white top and put his noise close to the opening. He breathed in a hooterful of its spicy odour. This was the only thing he bloody missed about England.

It had been something easily solved during Jackie's last trip home when she had followed his explicit and not-to-be-messed-about-with instructions about ordering a new supply. The memory of that visit started an unexpected avalanche of nasty thoughts in Gal's mind and suddenly he was picturing Jackie, drunk and desperate, being fucked by the Bastard-Monster-Logan. Probably in the back of a car somewhere. Probably in the back of his car.

The smell of burning bacon brought Gal back to the present and he hurriedly lifted the frying pan away from the heat.

'Grub's up!' he shouted to Don, who was wandering out on the patio having a fag.

'Fantastic!' pronounced Don, admiring the stacked plate of goodies that Gal had placed in front of him. 'You were always one for the grub, eh, Gal?'

Don grabbed the HP Sauce and patted the bottom of the bottle until a large dollop of the thick brown sauce oozed out. Gal watched Don stuffing his face with forkfuls of food and, for a moment, wondered if it was absolutely normal to cook a man breakfast an hour after he'd woken you up with a punch in the face. Gal decided that it probably was normal for people who knew Uncle Don.

While they ate, Gal suddenly saw that Enrique had appeared from nowhere. He was making himself busy sweeping up around the pool area. The fourteen-year-old was brushing far more vigorously than Gal could ever remember seeing him work before. Enrique was being careful not to look directly at Don at all, but he was clearly keeping a close eye on him nevertheless.

'You want more tea, Don?' asked Gal, seeing that the Bastard-Monster-Logan had emptied his mug.

'No, ta. It's all right. Maybe in a bit.'

The breakfast was beginning to revive Gal a little, as a good solid fry-up always did. He took another mouthful of egg and began convincing himself that Don Logan would be leaving the country today. Of course he would. How could he waste another twenty-four hours hanging around here waiting for a loser like Gal Dove to change his mind? Don was needed. Don was in charge (well, nearly). Don would, please, dear fucking God, have to go back soon.

The way Gal saw it, he just had to. Just a few more hours until lift-off. The countdown on Space Shuttle Bastard-Monster-Logan was set at less than twelve hours and counting.

'What was all that about?' said Don suddenly.

'What was all what about?'

'Why was Deedee going into one upstairs? She got herself into a right strop, didn't she? Women, eh?' snorted Don, sympathetically.

Twat.

'Well, Don, I think it's just that she doesn't like seeing her husband being woken up by getting punched full in the face by the house guest. She's funny like that. I know it might seem unreasonable when you think about it,' said Gal, not attempting to hide his sarcasm.

'All right. All right, I hear you,' said Don. Gal realized that this was probably as close to a normal human apology that Don ever got.

Gal took the empty plates from the table and dumped them into the sink. He made another two teas and took them out to Don, who was having another smoke in the morning sunshine on the patio. Keeping away from Don, but always in the background, was the figure of Enrique still sweeping the almost pristinely clean patio.

'I love you, Gal,' announced Don, as if this had come to him in a sudden, blinding revelation. 'You're lovable, you are. A big lovable bloke. A great lovable lump. A lovable lummox! Gal Dove – party boy! Big fucking oaf!'

Gal nodded in good-natured agreement.

'So how is she ... all right?' asked Don, knowingly.

'She's all right, yeah, thanks for asking,' agreed Gal.

Don raised his eyebrows in an exaggerated gesture that said, 'I bet she is.'

'All right, is she?'

'Oh fuck, here we go!' exclaimed Gal, getting up and moving away from Don.

'No, no. How is Deedee? Well, is she? She looks it – looking after herself – the climate obviously agrees with her. She still game for a laugh?' asked Don.

He was getting to it now. Earlier in the day than Gal had expected, but it was coming now.

Put it out of your mind. That was a different Deedee. Those things were not your Deedee.

Gal paced around the patio, unwilling to flee and unable to stay still.

'Honestly, when I think of all the birds you could've had and you had to pick her. Gal Dove. Gal fucking Dove. Dove the Love. Glamorous Gal! Gorgeous Gal! You used to have a great body. Great physique – handsome, you were. Birds loved you. Couldn't get enough, could they? But you had to go and end up with that ... Dirty Deedee.'

He's not saying anything you don't know already.

'I love her with all my heart,' said Gal, directly.

'You tosser!' said Don, slapping Gal straight back down. 'You don't know the half of it.'

You know what you need to know. It doesn't matter

what he says.

'I know what I need to know. I love her – that's it,' insisted Gal.

Gal walked towards Enrique and his constant, annoying brushing.

'You poor bastard! The things I could tell you – the shock would kill you! Do you know Vicky Raisins – the Maltese pornographer? Also known as Vicky Sultana?' continued Don.

Gal did not want Enrique to hear any of this.

'What did I tell you yesterday? Don't you ever listen?' shouted Gal, angrily interrupting the boy's cleaning. Enrique dropped his brush and scarpered over the patio wall, disappearing almost instantly.

'I don't want you here!' bellowed Gal after him.

Don continued with his train of thought as if nothing had happened. After all, he was just getting to the juicy bit.

'Of course, Old Vicky's an old man now. He's still operating, part-time these days. Just off the Old Kent Road he is now. He tells me that Deedee's still got a nice little fan club. They meet up the first Tuesday of every month – the Wednesday Wank, they call it.'

Shut up.

'Yeah, they're in big demand nowadays, those old super sixteens. She's still very popular, your wife. Very popular indeed. You seen any of them?'

An image pushed its way into Gal's mind. It was a picture of Deedee thirstily sucking on a large stiff cock while being taken from behind by another faceless male member. It was a picture of Deedee thrashing backwards and forwards while the men rode her like an animal, with more of them waiting in the wings to do exactly the same – and she was loving every single, filthy moment of it.

But the woman in Gal's picture wasn't the same Deedee as his lovely wife. The girl in the pictures was younger and different – not his Deedee at all. Gal knew all about her past film career, and he knew that that actress wasn't the Deedee he'd married. That wasn't the Deedee who he loved with all his heart and soul.

It had been a long time since Gal had thought about the old Deedee at all. He remembered one particular evening after a drinking session, when everyone had fallen into Ronnie's place and he had caught one of her films for the first time.

He'd known what she did even before they had met. The glamorous gangster and the porn star. It was too marvellous for words. Until that night at Uncle Ronnie's when he had walked into the noisy, smoky, alcohol-stinking back room and caught sight of Deedee being projected larger-than-life on to a grubby yellowed screen. A good-natured cheer went up around the room as three men came over her face at more or less the same time (allowing for understandable human error).

'I said, have you seen them?' pressed Don again, bringing Gal back to the present.

'Yeah, I've seen 'em.'

Don pulled a face, indicating that he'd seen them too and, not just that, but that he'd been morally offended by them as well.

'They're bad!' said Don, shaking his head. 'Ugly. She's doing everything in them. Everything.'

Shut up.

'Shut up, Don!'

'The worst ones of hers were that trilogy – there were

three of them, weren't there? *Planet of the Pussy-nymphs*, *Beneath the Planet of the Pussy-nymphs*, and *Escape from the Planet of the Pussy-nymphs*. It was every orifice! Deary me. What a stain on your love life, eh? All the Persil Automatic in the world wouldn't shift that! She's disgusting!'

Gal had heard enough. 'Be careful!' he threatened.

'What, have I said something wrong?' asked Don, innocently.

Upstairs in their bedroom, Deedee lay curled up on the bed. Their raised voices carried through the open windows and she could hear every stomach-turning word that came out of Don Logan's mouth. Every one of which tore another little piece of her new world to shreds.

'You're pathetic!' said Gal's voice.

'Am I?'

'I think so.'

'Do the job!'

'No!'

'Do the fucking job!'

'Fuck off!'

Gal headed into the kitchen with the excuse of taking the cups back inside. Really he just wanted to get away from Don for a moment. The tactic didn't work, though, as Don followed him inside like a shadow attached to the heels of its owner.

'Do it!' badgered Don.

'I'm retired!' Gal shouted back.

Of all the things that Gal had said, of all the excuses he had made up since Don had arrived at their villa, the word 'retired' seemed to be the most effective at making Don completely lose his rag.

'You say that fucking word once fucking more and I'm

gonna get a big fucking knife and stick it right in your fucking face! Do you understand me?' hissed Don, shaking with fury.

Gal said nothing and took his time putting the cups in the sink with the rest of the washing-up.

'Anyway, who do you two jokers think you are?' asked Don after a long pause. 'Who are you lording it up here in my fucking house?'

Gal couldn't believe his ears. 'What!?' he exclaimed, in stunned disbelief.

'This is my fucking house! Not yours. It's mine! It was paid for with my money, wasn't it? Money I gave you!' Don reasoned.

Gal was outraged. Even beyond the unnecessary description of the public entertainment value of his wife's many orifices, this was bang-fucking-out-of-order.

'Listen, I did nine years for that money. Nine fucking, shitty, miserable, cunting years!' he shouted.

Gal had done his duty and then some. He'd done nine solid years inside at Her Majesty's dull-grey-boring-life-wasting pleasure. Nine years rubbed out of the middle of his life. Every day the same, keys turning in locks, watch your back, lights out at seven same. Out of the whole team, they only had enough to make a case against Gal. Gorgeous Gal. Gorgeous pale-as-death-warmed-up-by-the-time-he-came-out Gal.

Of course, he could have been out in less than two years if he'd named names. If he'd squealed. But that wasn't Gal's style, was it? He was good old reliable Gal. You could trust Gal to keep his mouth shut. You could trust Gal to do nine years for you.

'You're swearing again! Do you want your little mouth

washed out with soap?'

'I earnt every penny of that fucking money!'

Don moved closer, dropping his voice. 'Yeah, but who looked after it while you were away? Who built up the interest on it? Moved it about, swelled it up for you?' he asked. 'Eh? Who? I did the honourable thing. I could have kept it – could have, but I didn't.'

'I earnt that fucking money. Once on the job, and once more inside,' insisted Gal.

'Do the job!'

'Find someone else!'

'I want you!'

'Don, I've had it with all that crime and punishment bollocks. I'm happy here!'

'I won't let you be happy,' threatened Don. 'Why should I? Why should you be happy?'

Silence.

Fuck you, Don Logan.

'I've told Ted you're doing it, so don't you show me up. Friday – the Grosvenor. Be there,' ordered Don.

'I'm not going,' said Gal.

'You will – you're Mr Rowntree! We can't do the job without Mr Rowntree, can we?'

'I won't be there, Don.'

'You will!'

'I won't!'

'Yes!'

'No!'

Don's face contorted into a wrinkled mask of frustration. 'Yes! Yes! Yes!'

Gal leaned back against the stove and saw how Don's body had transformed into a living knot of hatred.

'Look, Don, let's not kid ourselves,' Gal heard himself saying. 'We both know the reason why you're here. And it's not just because of me.'

Don couldn't have looked more surprised and shocked if he'd just taken a bullet between the eyes. He almost staggered back, shocked beyond belief by what Gal had just dared to say. For the first time since his arrival, Don was speechless.

Gal wasn't sure if what he'd said was going to turn out to be very very clever or very very stupid.

'What,' said Don, still flabbergasted, 'the fuck are you actually saying?'

16. Uncle Don's problem

with authority figures

Gal Dove wondered whether he was about to die, or if perhaps he had just saved his own life.

'Let's be honest ...' he said to the still-stunned Don.

'What are you talking about?' said Don, eyes widening in innocence.

Gal began to feel that he was on firmer ground and decided to press home any advantage he had.

'Come on, Don. This isn't just about me,' Gal suggested again.

Don was rocked back in his tracks once again.

'I'm finding this astonishing. This is amazing. You're astounding me,' he said, struggling to find words to express his utter disbelief.

'You didn't just come here because of me, did you, Don?' insisted Gal.

'Am I losing the plot here? I think that I must be losing the plot or something,' spluttered Don.

Don was clearly unsure how to play this and uncertain of what he should do next. 'Look, Gal, I don't know exactly what you're going on about . . .' he began.

Don's body posture and the tone of his voice said quite the opposite, however. Don's body posture and the tone of his voice said, 'ARRGGGGGHH! This is the most difficult and embarrassing subject that you could ever mention, you cunt-faced bastard. I cannot fucking deal with this.'

' . . .And to be quite frank with you,' Don continued, 'I'm not exactly interested in whatever it is. But I will say this – I've come over here for professional reasons. Nothing else. I'm on a professional mission. I've got to get a team together. I've got to carefully hand-pick a team. I did have you in mind for a part in that team – but quite frankly your attitude appals me!'

The fact that he now appalled Don was the best piece of news that Gal could possibly have had. If, that is, he was going to live to tell it to anybody.

'It's not what you're saying that bothers me, it's all the stuff you're not saying – insinuendoes!' said Don, inventing a useful new word. 'You really are demonstrating some whopping great ego, my friend, and I'd keep that in check if I were you 'cos that sort of big-headedness can be a right turn-off! Now, if you don't want to do the job – fair enough – I can accept that. We'll leave it at that . . . considering what I know about you and the outrageousness of what's going on inside your head. Whatever stinking thoughts you're having, I don't wish to know about because they're so disgusting, and I would like to leave – now – this minute. Please get me a taxi,' he finally finished.

Fantastic.

For a second Gal didn't know what to say. 'Sorry, Don?'

'I should like a taxi, please, to take me away from this place.'

Do it. Do it. Quickly. Do it!

Gal's mind froze with English politeness. The first rule of Polite English Society, even Gangster Society, is that a host never lets his guest leave in a huff. Even if said host desperately wants said guest to fuck off to the ends of the earth, he still has to go through the motions of politeness and say the opposite of what he means:

Things like, 'No, no, Don, I didn't mean it. I'm sorry, we'd love you to at least stay for lunch.'

Or, 'Don, I unreservedly apologize for that last remark. I should, in fact, be delighted to do this bank job with you. Please forget what I said about not wanting to serve any more time inside just because you might arse this job up, like the last one we did together.'

Gal's mind quickly worked its way through all the possibilities and one-third of a second later he said:

'I'll call you a cab.'

When he rang to order the taxi, Gal wasn't confident enough of his Spanish to attempt the phrase, 'Fucking immediately and with extreme urgency as if my life depended on it, please,' so he just asked for it 'as soon as you can.'

It seemed to do the trick, and about thirty minutes later Gal watched as the cab pulled out of his driveway heading towards the airport. The solitary passenger in the back seat sat stiffly upright, staring straight ahead.

From one of the upstairs windows, Deedee watched the car until it became just a dot in the distance before it dropped over the horizon and disappeared out of sight completely.

Don had hardly said another word since his request for the cab. He had disappeared up to the guest room and only emerged when he heard the taxi honking outside.

'I hope he knows I haven't got all day,' Don said, nodding towards the waiting taxi driver.

'Goodbye, Don,' said Gal, offering his hand.

'Yeah,' answered Don, extending his own hand then, at the last second, raising it to his face, putting the thumb on his nose and wiggling his fingers at Gal like a naughty eight-year-old.

Fucker.

Don had already decided that not having Gal on the job was the best thing that ever happened to him in the whole of his life. Ever.

'Fat fucking blob,' Don had cursed under his breath during the taxi ride. 'Fucking fat git. Fucking balloon. He looks like someone's taken a bicycle pump to him and not known when to stop. He could join the Roly Polys now – free life membership. He's a fucking freak! Fucking hippo. Dear oh dear – put him in a sideshow and he'd frighten the kids. People would demand their money back!'

Less than an hour later, Don Logan was sitting in the departure lounge of the airport – although the term was, perhaps, a rather grand way to describe the few rows of uncomfortable plastic chairs in which travellers waited for their plane.

A franchise coffee stand called 'CUPPA COFFEE' sold lukewarm watery drinks to unwary punters. Someone had obviously wised up at some point in the recent past because a thick black marker pen had been used to change the name of the stand to 'CRAPPA COFFEE'.

Don had already decided against having any of the foreign muck. He'd wait until he was home in London for a decent brew.

Although the departure lounge was crowded with

holiday-makers returning home after baking themselves stupid on Spanish beaches, the two chairs on either side of Don stayed noticeably empty. This was because although Don Logan was deep in silent thought, occasionally the odd abusive sentence would pop out aloud without him being aware of it.

'No, he's a cunt,' Don twitched aloud more than once.

Don's brain was on overdrive, running through the extensive list of candidates who could replace Gal on the next night's exciting episode of Criminal Mission Impossible. There was no shortage of contestants – the trouble was, they were mostly cunts of one kind or another.

Who was there really? Who had the capabilities for a big job like this one? There was Edgar – nah, fuck him. He was a bit of a liar; if he was on the job you couldn't believe a bloody word that came out of his mouth. That fucker could lie for England.

Trevor Morris? Definitely not, he was a king-sized wanker. He wasn't worth even one per cent of a job. There was old Granger ... How old was he now, though? Probably beyond-a-joke old. Probably in-a-bloody-bathchair old.

Who else? Not Welshie, that's for sure. He was a ...

'Fucking nut,' said Don aloud.

Several brightly-dressed holiday-makers shifted uneasily in their seats and pulled their annoying-brat-wanting-ice-cream-again-already-children away from Don.

Don continued his internal deliberations until the passengers on the 14.15 flight to Heathrow were herded across the runway like goats. Don took his place next to a large Spanish woman whose extensive body seemed to ooze into Don's own seat in a warm and flabby invasion of unwanted flesh.

Now he could return to his mental list. What about Barney? Did he have the bottle for it? Had he got the bollocks? On balance, fucking no, he didn't. Anyway, the last thing you wanted along on a big job was a shitter. They'd just scare the shit out of everyone else as well as themselves.

But Roy Sumpter? He could hack it. He's a good boy, he's smart and strong – very important things. He's loyal too. Yeah, there were lots worse choices than Roy Sumpter. It's Roy. It could fucking well be Roy.

Don could imagine the conversation.

'You interested in a shit-load of money, Roy?'

''Course I am, Don.'

'You wanna do a big, juicy cunt of a job with me, Roy?'

''Course I do, Don. What kind of wanker wouldn't want to do a big, juicy cunt of a job, especially with you?'

It was Roy.

Don was a happy man and knew that, having made such a good and solid choice, he could finally sit back and enjoy the flight home, where a huge tasty bank job and a huge, grateful Roy would be waiting for him.

'It's Roy!' said Don aloud.

To celebrate his decision, Don reached into his shirt pocket and took out his packet of fags. He pushed open the lid, took a brown filter between his lips and flicked his lighter into life. He took a deep drag into his lungs and relaxed.

Fucking fat boy Gal. Who needs him?

A tall stewardess with her dark hair hidden under a blue and yellow cap came towards Don down the aisle of the aircraft.

'Sir, I'm afraid you cannot smoke. The "No Smoking" sign is on.'

Don was lost in thoughts of a blissfully executed job.

'What? Whaddya want?'

'Sir, you have to put out your cigarette ... please.'

What was the world coming to if a man couldn't have a fag in the privacy of his own plane?

'Cigarette? What – this?' said Don, waving the offending fag towards her cheek-boned face. 'No, I'm not going to put it out.'

'You must,' ordered the young woman, not used to having her authority challenged by a pleb holiday-maker.

Don wasn't having any of it. 'Why's that? Why have I got to put it out? What harm am I doing you?'

'If you do not put it out then we cannot take off ...' explained the stewardess, sure of the strength of her logic.

'Well, that's your problem, ain't it? You're the ones flying the bleeding plane, not me.'

Don took another drag of his ciggie and stared up at her as if to say, 'Your move, love.'

'Please, sir,' she tried again.

'Nah, I ain't putting it out. You're gonna have to wait until I finished it – simple as that,' said Don, loudly.

He took another long puff, while the frustrated stewardess returned up the aisle seeking help and advice.

'Look, why don't you just put the cigarette out?' said a man's voice from the row immediately behind Don.

Fucking outrage.

Don looked round.

'What's that, Long Nose? Do you want me to cut off your hand and use it as an ashtray? Yeah, I'll put it out, mate, if you're prepared to let me stub it out in your eyeball. I'll put it out then. Are you agreeable?'

Strangely the man sitting behind didn't seem too keen on

Don's idea and shut up. When Don turned around from dealing with the prat behind he saw the stewardess returning down the aisle accompanied by two stewards.

'Oh, here comes the gay brigade.' Don quickly slid out of his seat. 'I'll tell you what, I'll get off the plane, eh?'

He snapped open the overhead baggage compartment, and grabbed out his bag. Then he pushed straight past the stewardess and marched down the aisle towards the exit.

'I'll fucking get off again. You happy with that? I'm happy with that! I'll smoke my cigarette outside!'

At the open door of the exit, Don paused and turned back to face the other passengers.

'I hope it crashes!' he said.

17. 'I was most perturbed'

When Carlos Rizza was first told the story of the cigarette-smoking tosser who delayed and then decided to leave the 14.15 flight to England, he thought it was a wind-up. When he realized that the story was for real, he was delighted.

Since leaving the plane and climbing down the mobile airport steps, Don Logan, the cigarette-smoking tosser in question, had been escorted by about half the airport's entire security squad into the police holding room.

Carlos was told of his arrival and the incident that led to it immediately, but left Mr Logan to stew for some considerable time before seeing him.

The police holding room was a bare and empty room that offered its prisoners no points of interest whatsoever. Don had spent most of his time there pacing the floor and, when he was bored with that, sitting at the bare wooden table. To the right and left of the door stood two large and armed Spanish policemen in immaculate uniforms.

The door opened and Don looked up with renewed interest as Carlos Rizza entered. He was carrying Don's passport and papers. He pulled out a chair and sat opposite Don.

'This is very serious, Mr Logan.'

'You're right, sir. This is very serious. I've been sitting here for five hours!' said Don, keeping his voice low and calm.

This was Carlos's chance to play bad cop and he didn't want be interrupted.

'As you may know, all European airlines are subject to ...'

'Look, before you start, I want to say something,' said Don, interrupting the man who didn't want to be interrupted. 'Have you ever been sexually assaulted?' Don continued, leaning forward to speak in hushed tones. 'No, neither have I – until today – on that plane.'

What?

'What?'

'Yeah, that's what I said. Here's me putting my bag in the cupboard, next thing you know I feel hands on me! Someone's touched me – touched my front bottom! I can't believe it. I've gone cold all over. I've looked round and he's standing there, isn't he? The steward with a guilty look on his face. Well, I was shocked!'

The conversation was not going at all how Carlos had imagined that it would.

'I didn't know what to say! I had to sit down. I was most perturbed. And now his mate, the other one, who's giving us all lessons on what to do if we crash in the sea and that, now he starts as well! He starts looking at me all funny, suggestive like. I don't know if they wanted me for a two's up or something ...'

Carlos tried to think of something to say.

'I don't know how they work it, but I tell you what, it scared me! I was shaking like a leaf. So I lit up a cigarette to calm me down. I was trembling. I was very emotional ...

and that's when the rest of it happened. It's very regrettable,' protested Don.

That much Carlos could agree with.

'Now, I'd rather not kick up a fuss, press charges, contact the British Embassy. I'd rather not pursue those channels. It's not my style – I'm not that sort of bloke. I wouldn't want to lose the man his job. A man's gotta eat, and I'm sure he's not representative of all Spanish people, but I would appreciate it if you'd have a word with him. Let him know he's been rumbled.'

Carlos swallowed hard. This wasn't at all how he'd imagined things would turn out.

Don leaned towards him.

'It was the one with the ginger hair,' he offered confidentially. 'Can I go now, please?'

18. Things get unpleasant

As Gal lay soaking in a warm bath, he imagined himself doing a length of his swimming pool, powering his way through the sun-warmed water. In a few days his pool would be repaired and everything in his life would be back exactly the way that it had been before – exactly the way he wanted it.

Part of Gal couldn't believe that getting rid of Don had been so easy. 'Easy' being a relative term, though, for twenty-four hours of hell, a punch in the face, a dead-leg, constant verbal assault, dragging up your wife's sordid past and pissing on the bathroom floor. Still, they were all alive, Don was gone, and soon, very soon, Gal would have his lovely pool back.

Gal's hunger finally overcame his urge to stay in the bath for the entire evening and he pulled out the plug with his right foot. As he finished dressing in his grey silk suit, Aitch joined him in the bedroom.

'He'll be landing in London about now,' said Aitch, consulting his watch. 'And I'll you something, there's no way in the entire world that he'll be telling them the truth.'

'Well, what will he say, then? I'm not doing it, am I?'

'No, you're not doing it, but what, you think he's saying – "Gal told me to go and fuck myself so I came straight home. Sorry, lads, your Uncle Don's let you down"? You think he's gonna say that?'

Gal faced the mirror and began combing through his still-damp hair.

'Come on, Gal! How long are you gonna be?' Deedee's agitated voice called from downstairs where she was waiting to start their meal.

'Two seconds, I'm combing my hair!' he shouted back.

'If Don said that, he'd look a right cunt, wouldn't he?' continued Aitch.

'That's exactly what he is,' Gal reminded him.

Aitch realized that he was not getting his point across.

'That's not what I'm saying. I'm saying that he has to save face, doesn't he? Protect himself, his image, his ego.'

Gal and Aitch began making their way downstairs to where the girls were waiting to eat.

'Now, I'll tell you what's happened,' continued Aitch. 'This is what I'd do. He's gone back and he's said, "I've decided not to go with Gal – he's far too fat!"'

'Fuck off!' said Gal playfully.

'He's put on a ton of weight and he looks like the fucking Michelin man!' said Aitch.

'I am fucking beautiful, I am,' said Gal, patting his ample waistline. 'I'm lovely.'

'Of course, you are, mate,' agreed Aitch kindly, 'but you've got to put your mind into his perspective. See things the way he sees things. You're right in the clear, trust me.'

Even before the words 'trust me' had left Aitch's mouth, both he and Gal were aware of the sound of speeding wheels coming up the driveway. Visitors at this time of night were exceedingly rare. Fuck it, they just never happened. Gal and Aitch looked at each other in horror.

No, please, fucking no.

'Gal!'

Deedee's urgent voice called him from her place out on the patio. Gal rushed out to see Deedee and Jackie getting out of their chairs and backing away from . . . Don.

Oh shit.

Don's eyes were wild with hate.

'Do you think I'm stupid? Think I'm some kind of fucking cunt? Some fucking twat?!' he shouted in their general direction.

Behind him, the cab driver swiftly turned his yellow taxi around and headed away as quickly as he could. It had clearly not been a relaxing journey for him, and now that his passenger had got out he made a swift escape.

'Think I'm gonna have that? Do you really think I'm gonna have that? My fucking ears were burning, all the way back in the fucking car. They were fucking on fire!'

Gal was gobsmacked by Don's unexpected and most cuntish return.

'What happened, Don?'

Don seemed like a man possessed. He was about one inch away from killing someone, that was for sure. His body was shaking with unreleased fury.

'What happened? What fucking happened?? I'll tell you what fucking happened! You gave me a fucking knock-back, you fat, fucking cunt!' bellowed Don, half-paralyzed with rage.

Gal tried to think of something to say that might take the heat out of Don's anger. He couldn't.

'Problem with the plane, Don?' said Aitch, meekly.

Not a good idea.

Don rounded on him with extreme hatred.

'What's that? What did you fucking say? Cunt! What fucking problem? No, mate, no! No problem with the fucking plane, you cunt! Fucking plane was fine. Fucking plane was all right. Fucking plane was perfect. It's *you*!'

Aitch wanted to back away, but Don's eyes held him as if in a vice-like grip and Aitch couldn't shift his gaze.

'*You're* the problem! *You're* the fucking problem! You fucking Dr White! You fucking spunk bubble! I'm telling you, Aitch, you keep looking at me and I'm gonna put you in the fucking ground – I promise you!'

Aitch looked down at the ground. Anywhere but at Don.

'Deedee, why don't you take Jackie and Aitch inside?' suggested Gal urgently.

'Can I get you something to drink, Don?' offered Deedee, her voice smooth and calm as she shepherded the others into the villa.

Don didn't reply, but continued to stare at Aitch's back.

'Yeah, go and hide, you scheming cunt! See if the ladies'll let you try on one of their panty-girdles while you're in there!' he called after the retreating figure.

With the others safely indoors, Gal and Don were left alone on the patio.

'Don . . .' began Gal, but he didn't get very far.

The bald man rounded on him again, still full of fury.

Fuck.

'Shut up! Just shut up! Just fucking shut up!'

Don paced up and down the patio, his head full of furious thoughts which Gal knew were about to flood out.

'Not this time, Gal! Not this time! Not this fucking time! No. No! No, no, no, no, no, no, no! Not this fucking time! No fucking way! You've made me look a right cunt! Like a right fucking Mr Confused. What's he doing? What's Jackie gonna think to that? Not that I care any more! I'm not into her any more!'

At the mention of her name, Jackie moved uncomfortably where she was sitting just inside the house.

'I've just realized,' continued Don, pointing his finger at Gal, 'that this is all your fault. Fucking me about. Is your middle name "Ungrateful" or something? Ain't you got anything to say? You just gonna stand there like Porky Pig hiding behind your wife's skirt? Your ex-porn star wife's skirt!'

Don lowered his voice slightly, but it was a great struggle for Don to say anything at a low volume.

'I don't give two fucks what Jackie Big-tits thinks of me coming back! She can think what she likes! I've got enough fucking information on her! So what if she's got a pretty face – that can all change. Age changes that! I wanna see her when she's seventy! Let's see if she's still coming the cunt with a face like a wrinkled prune! I can't fucking wait! Aitch'll be well gone by then of course.'

Don threw a disgusted glance inside the house and saw Aitch, Jackie and Deedee peering through the glass of the patio doors, heads bowed, waiting for Hurricane Don to dissipate.

Don looked over at Gal and saw that he was waiting as well. Waiting to see what Don would do next. Gal hadn't apologized. He hadn't begged Don to let him in on the job. He still hadn't realized what an ungrateful little cunt he had actually been. In that moment, Don realized that he hated Gal. He hated his fat belly. He hated his sunny new life in Dago-land. And he hated him not being interested any more.

'I'm gonna kill you, Gal,' announced Don with surprising calm.

He turned to face towards the house and said, 'I'm gonna fucking kill him!'

Don reached quickly but calmly over and picked up an empty beer bottle from the patio table. In a smooth and very professional motion, Don brought the heavy glass bottle smashing down on to Gal's skull.

'Jesus!'

Inside the house, Deedee screamed.

Gal stumbled back, crimson liquid gushing from the deep wound. He fell over, crashing hard into the unforgiving concrete of the patio. Don advanced, ready to inflict more damage and enjoying the thought of what he might get up to next.

To Gal's surprise, Don stopped moving. His attention had been attracted by something moving around the side of the house. Gal looked up to see Enrique walking slowly out of the darkness towards Don. The boy looked utterly terrified, his movements were jerky and his arms were shaking with fear. In his hands was his father's ancient rifle which he was pointing squarely at Don's chest.

Enrique looked close to tears, but continued walking until he had placed himself in between Gal and Bastard-Monster-Logan. Gal was still groggy from the blow, but saw clearly enough what was happening.

'Enrique, no! Go home!' he ordered, clutching at his head wound.

Don's face erupted into a broad grin.

'What? You pointing a gun at me?' he said, evidently enjoying himself.

'Go home, son!' urged Gal again.

Enrique was breathing hard.

'You pointing a gun at me?' Don repeated.

Aitch and Jackie came out of the house and on to the patio. For some reason, Deedee had deserted them – suddenly disappeared upstairs.

Don took a slow and deliberate step towards the shaking Enrique.

'What, you gonna shoot me? Eh? Are ya? You gonna shoot me?' he taunted. 'Go on then – shoot! It's all right, I don't mind. Shoot me, why not?'

Don was loving it. He moved even closer to Enrique. The boy's teeth were now chattering with blind fear.

'You cold? Bit cold out here for you? Tell you what, I'll have that!'

Don reached forward and gently but firmly grasped the barrel of the gun. He slid it out of the boy's hands with no resistance, leaving Enrique holding an invisible rifle.

Don dropped his smile.

'Don't you ever, ever, ever point a gun at me again,' he ordered, sternly. With one swift movement, Don brought the stock of the rifle swinging across Enrique's forehead, dealing him a nasty blow. The boy fell to the ground.

'There you go,' smiled Don. He moved back towards Gal, who was still on the ground nursing his bleeding head. Behind them, Deedee appeared in the doorway of the kitchen, and in her hands was a long tube of dangerous shiny metal.

Don balled his fist and stepped towards Gal.

19. One of our cunts is missing

London. Rain slapped down on the roof of the black cab sounding like slabs of meat hitting a floor. Sitting morosely alone on the spacious back seat of the cab was Gal Dove. A large Elastoplast plaster covered the area just behind his ear. Every now and then his hand was drawn unconsciously up to his neck to check that the dressing was still in place.

The taxi's windscreen wipers worked furiously to swipe water away from the glass.

'Lovely, ain't it?' called the driver from his perch on the edge of his front seat. 'It's been like this all week.'

Gal stared out at the weather like a condemned man.

'You been on holiday then, mate?' asked the driver, spotting that Gal's heavy tan was rather incongruous with the bleak and unforgiving weather of his current surroundings.

'Italy,' lied Gal. 'My brother was marrying an Italian bird, wasn't he?'

'Lucky bastard,' smiled the driver, signalling to pull over.

Gal saw that they'd arrived. The large brick building of the Grosvenor Hotel stretched up towards the dirty grey heavens.

'That's twenty-six quid, forty pence,' said the driver. 'You wanna receipt?'

Under any other circumstances, Gal would have balked at the price, but he had other things on his mind. He handed over a ten and a twenty pound note and didn't wait for change.

As he opened the cab door, a sheet of rain blasted inside. Droplets hit his desert sand suit, staining the material with dark watery spots. Gal ran from the taxi towards the hotel. He could not remember England being this cold.

Gal walked up to reception.

'I believe,' he said, 'you have a reservation for a Mr Rowntree?'

The receptionist checked the already open book on the desk, then looked up with a welcoming smile. Indeed they did.

The first thing that Gal did when he had been left alone in hotel room was to open the mini-bar and stare sadly at its contents. What Gal felt like doing was getting blind drunk, but he knew he couldn't. Having tortured himself with a long gaze at the booze on offer, Gal decided on a shower to warm himself up instead.

Unfortunately, it was one uncomfortable hotel shower; Gal could only stand about ten minutes under its high-pressure water spray which battered his skin with needle-like ferocity. Afterwards, he sat wrapped in a bath towel, dripping on to his bed. Room service delivered a turkey and salad sandwich and he miserably nibbled his way through it, washing it down with the contents of a miniature whisky bottle. (Just the one, mind.)

At 7.12, the phone on the bedside table rang. Gal snatched it up.

'Hello?'

'Mr Rowntree, we have a call for you,' said the voice of the hotel receptionist.

A second later there was a click and another voice came on the line.

'Is that Mr Rowntree?' said a voice, darkly.

'Yes,' said Gal, wary of everything.

'Hello, Mr Rowntree. You all right for later?' it asked.

'Yeah,' said Gal.

'You know where you're going?'

'No.'

'Doesn't matter. Mike does, he's your driver, all right?'

'OK.'

'Is that Gal?' said the voice, suddenly dropping the cloak and dagger act.

'Who's that? Is that Stan?'

'Yeah, fucking hell, how're you, Gal? You're doing it? Last time I spoke to Logan the Shogun he wasn't sure you'd be up for it!' chirped the very recognizable Stan Higgins.

'No, I'm up for it. I'm up for it all right,' said Gal grimly.

'Nice one. Listen, mate, I've got a lot of calling to do. We'll see you later, all right?' said Stan.

'I'll be there,' said Gal. 'Like I've got a fucking choice,' he muttered to himself as he replaced the receiver.

Just over an hour later another voice from reception told him, in slightly disapproving tones, that there was 'a Mike' waiting by the desk for him.

Gal finished dressing and ten minutes later was sitting in Mike's car, once more being driven through London. Mike had another pick-up to make at the Savoy Hotel, where Jimmy and Peter joined Gal in the rear of the vehicle. They sat in silence while Mike drove through northeast London and out into what became the Essex countryside.

Many country lanes later, it seemed to Gal that they had

finally reached the middle of nowhere. If nowhere had a middle, then the dilapidated World War II hangar in front of Gal in the silent, wet, cold, pitch-black countryside was surely it.

Gal followed Jimmy, Peter and Mike into the cavernous interior. A few dim lamps provided the minimal lighting. At the far end of the hangar, a group of men were gathered around a trestle table on which were laid out sets of plans – all of them the worse for wear – covered in grubby finger-marks and coffee stains. A half-empty case of beer sat at the end of the table.

In the gloom, Gal saw two sets of clothes rails, on which were hanging half a dozen wet suits. On the rough, concrete floor in front of the wet suits was a large, dirty plastic sheet, where several bright yellow oxygen tanks and some drilling equipment were placed.

Gal looked round at the faces moving about the hangar. Some were strangers, but he recognized Dermot – a great tall tosser who must have gambled away everything he'd ever made from his criminal career. Behind him was Raymond, with his great tall forehead looking like an alien from *Star Fucking Trek: The Geek Generation*. Talking to him was Bruno, who seemed to have lost about fifteen stone since Gal last saw him.

'The wet suits are all coming in a bit small,' said Dermot. 'Allow a bit extra on all of them, OK?' he told Raymond.

In a darkened corner of the hangar, Gal's eyes found Teddy Bass, well dressed and suave as ever, standing with Stan Higgins and Malky Logan. Malky was Don's brother and the family resemblance was enough to make Gal stop in his tracks for a moment.

'He's treating me like a cunt, Malky! Does he think I'm a cunt?' Teddy was asking.

'I'm not arguing with you, Ted. I agree . . .'

Teddy stared murderously at Malky. 'Does he think I'm a cunt?'

'I'm with you, Ted. I'll kill him my fucking self when I see him!'

Malky looked over to Stan, who merely shrugged his shoulders; clearly he had no answers either. Then he caught sight of Gal.

'Gal, you got a minute?' he called across the hangar.

Gal hesitated for a split second, then approached the gang of three.

'Ted! Stan! Malky!'

'Wotcha, Gal!' greeted Malky.

There was an awkward silence for a couple of seconds, then Stan spoke as if he was bringing up a sad and very personal matter in public and that he very much regretted even having to mention it.

'How did he seem, Gal? How did he come across? Was he all right?' asked Stan.

'Who?'

The question didn't really need asking.

'Don.'

'Oh, Don. Yeah, he was all right. He's Don, ain't he? Why?' said Gal.

Teddy and Stan exchanged looks. Teddy's said, 'Tell him.'

Here we go.

'We're just trying to trace his movements. He was due back in London on Wednesday,' explained Stan.

'He missed that plane. We were talking about stuff – old

times and the job and that. Went out drinking,' offered Gal. 'He stayed at mine on Wednesday night. Left on Thursday.'

'Yesterday?' said Stan.

'Yeah, that's what I meant,' said Gal.

'Did you drop him off at the airport?' asked Stan.

Bloody twenty questions or what?

'No, he got a cab – why?'

'So you didn't actually see him get on the plane?' Stan quizzed him.

'Well, no, not personally, but I know he did.'

Teddy Bass, who had almost drifted away from the conversation, suddenly turned back to Gal.

'How?'

'Because ... because he called me from Heathrow,' Gal lied, feeling the pressure.

'He called you?'

Shit. What a stupid thing to say. When did Don Logan ever call you? Fucker.

'Yeah, he called me. Why, what's happened?' said Gal, committed.

Play for time.

'Why did he call you?' demanded Teddy. 'What did he say?'

'I dunno. He said he'd landed safely ... I thought it was a bit funny myself ...'

Excellent recovery.

'No, he would do that,' chimed Malky in the nick of time. 'It's the sort of thing he would do – just being hospitable. Thanking Gal for putting him up and that, eh, Gal?'

Yeah, like your rude, fucked-up, dead brother would call anyone if he didn't want something for himself. Like he'd call to say 'thank you'.

Teddy began staring at Malky once again and Stan quickly shepherded Gal away.

'Sorry about this, Gal. It's just that Don's gone AWOL. Obviously it's a matter for concern, as I'm sure you'll appreciate – but we'll get there. Too much time and money has gone into this for it to be fucked around by one cunt's strangeness,' explained Stan. 'I'm glad you're on board, Gal. No one can touch you for this sort of thing. Go and have a drink with the others, and we'll be over in a minute to take you all through the whole thing.' He pointed Gal in the direction of the case of beer.

As Gal began to walk across the gloomy hangar floor, he caught sight of something in his memory. Pushing itself to the forefront of his mind was a vision of Don Logan. It was a vision of Don's entire stomach exploding with a loud bang. It was a vision of bits of blood and tissue propelling themselves outwards, like an alien baby bursting from its host.

It was Don looking down at the messy red cavity where his stomach had once been and collapsing. It was Don squirming on the ground, writhing in agony, struggling to get up, with half his stomach shot away and a pool of warm, sticky blood colouring the patio around him ...

20. Die-fucking-hard

Shit.

Gal looked over to the villa and saw Deedee standing in the kitchen doorway. In her trembling hands was Gal's shotgun.

Oh fuck.

Don was on the floor. It was clear from the expression on his face that the part of being shot he was finding hardest was believing that it had actually happened. Any way he looked at it, Don just couldn't fucking believe it.

He looked down at the massive hole where his stomach should have been and whimpered. His arms and legs jerked in uncontrollable spasms as he thrashed around in pain.

Gal, with blood still streaming down his neck from his head wound, watched Don's contortions with astonishment. Jackie ran over to the unconscious Enrique, sprawled nearby, and checked that he was still breathing. He was. She cradled the boy's head in her arms and patted his cheek, gently trying to bring him round.

Deedee still stood in the kitchen doorway, her body appearing hunched and exhausted.

Don, on the other hand, was beginning to realize what

had happened to him and was unintelligibly cursing and swearing. He moved his limbs in an effort to struggle to his feet, but his fatally wounded body offered him no support.

'You shot me! You fucking shot me!' he spluttered in vein-popping rage. 'You cunts! Dirty fucking cunt animals! I'm gonna fucking kill you!'

Then, suddenly, he seemed to realize just how fucked he really was.

'Help me! Oh, my God, someone fucking help me! Criminals! I been shot!' he howled.

Gal pulled himself to his feet and staggered over to where Don was dying. He leant down and began to methodically deliver heavy punches to Don's head.

'You see? You see? You treat my wife with respect!' he screamed.

Don didn't take kindly to this new assault.

'You're punching my fucking head!' he yelled.

Gal was becoming hysterical. Tears filled his eyes as he assailed Don with blow after blow.

'She's beautiful! She's beautiful! You dirty cunt! She's beautiful!' he sobbed.

'Aitch, help me, you cunt!' called Don, with a note of apology in his voice. 'You rotten fucking bastards!'

Don reached up and managed to grab hold of Gal's neck as he delivered yet another blow. The two were now stuck in a bloody, scruffy, grappling match. Seeing the injured Gal in Don's messy grip spurred Deedee into action again. She waded into the fight, punching and kicking whatever parts of Don she could reach. Just behind her, Jackie came across the patio, ready to join in as well.

'Jackie, I love you!' said Don, almost incomprehensible

through the bubbling, frothy blood that was leaking from his mouth.

Jackie lashed out, kicking Don in what little remained of his ribs. Don swung his leg and scored a lucky hit on her, knocking her to the floor. She landed roughly, but her hatred was so great that the pain didn't interrupt her continued kicking of Don. Don tried to grab her foot, but her white stiletto came off in his bloody hand.

'I love you!' panted Don, through his immense pain.

Jackie's foot smashed into his face, breaking his nose.

'You don't tear my life apart! You don't tear my life apart!' screamed Deedee, still pummelling Don's upper chest.

'You've fucked hundreds! Hundreds!' he shouted back at her face.

Gal lost it completely. 'You cunt! I'm gonna fucking kill you!' he said, grabbing Don's neck in a stranglehold.

'Kill me? Kill me? Cocksucker! I'll fucking kill you!'

Jackie added her hands to Gal's, but Don was proving very hard to kill.

'You're dead, Gal! You're fucking dead! Murdering cunts! Wankers,' gasped Don through the onslaught.

'Aitch, get the fucking gun!' cried Jackie, urgently.

But Aitch, stunned by the ugly, clumsy, punching, dragging, kicking heap of bodies in front of him, did not move. Instead, it was Deedee who extricated herself from the violent mess, crawled over to the gun and picked it up. She pushed the twin barrels into Don's chest and fired.

Jackie and Gal reeled back, exhausted.

Don was panting heavily, his limbs twitching. He struggled to focus on the shapes moving around him.

'Fucking joke. Fucking jokers!' he hissed weakly. 'Think that's funny, do you? Oh, bollocks ...'

He caught sight of Gal and attempted a two-fingered 'V' sign, but found that he could no longer move his arm.

'Up the Hammers!' he managed.

Recognizing that the bastard was probably about two seconds away from dying, Aitch finally approached, carrying the heavy metal tray of the barbecue. Don stared up into his face.

'I fucked Jackie. Fucked her. Ask her – she'll tell you. I fucked her!' Don spat weakly, in a final act of spite.

Jackie's guilty face told its own story.

Aitch raised the metal barbecue base over his head.

'Yeah, well, I've just fucked you, though, haven't I?' he growled, bringing the metal base clattering down on to Don's head, splitting his skull in two.

21. The jolly boys' Chinese beano

Gal decided that perhaps this was better than sitting alone and shitting yourself all evening after all. But only just.

All the boys, except Teddy and Stan, were sitting around a large round table in Marx's Chinese Restaurant in Chinatown. Going out with the lads had been the last thing Gal had felt like doing when he'd been invited, but he really couldn't get out of it. And anyway, he had fuck-all else to do apart from shit bricks about tomorrow's job.

They were on their main course, and each time one of the lads finished the food on one plate, a waiter's arm would appear to whisk the empty bowl away and replace it with another, brimming with Oriental delights.

'You eating that, Gal, or what?' asked Pete, who was sitting next to him. Gal scooped half a dozen sweet and sour prawns out of the serving dish and passed it to Pete.

'It's not the first time that this has happened, ya know?' said Malky, Don's very-slightly-less-psychotic brother.

'No?'

'Don was always fucking doing it when we were kids. I remember one time when Mum sent him up the shops for a tin of fruit – pears or peaches or something. Anyway, he never came back for two days!' Malky told them. 'He had to when he got really hungry. It turned out that Don had gone up the arcade with the money and blown it! He was too scared to come home, 'cause he knew that Mum would cut his arse!'

The table erupted into laughter. Gal did his best to smile along, trying to keep out of his mind the image of Don's brains leaking all over his patio.

'Here, Gal, I saw that bloke the other day. The one who knows you? The one with the blond hair,' said Pete, through a mouthful of lemon rice.

'Who's that?'

'The one you used to hang around with. Big bloke – tall, blond hair . . .' described Pete.

'I don't know who you mean,' said Gal.

'Yeah, you do,' continued Pete, shovelling in another spoonful of food. 'You used to knock about with him ages ago. Anyway, he was asking after you. Blond fella. You must know who I'm talking about. He's got very blond hair!'

Gal's face was blank. 'Pete, I'm sorry mate, I can't think who you mean.'

'Yes, you do. You do. You know this bloke well. I don't know how else to say it. He's got blond hair. I met him and you know him!' insisted Pete.

'What colour hair's he got?' asked Mike, dryly.

'Blond. Shut up!' snapped Pete, then he turned back to Gal. 'What's his name? What's his fucking name?'

'Pete, I can't help you, mate!' shrugged Gal.

'Well, anyway, I met the blond bloke that you know and he says, "Hello",' said Pete, exasperated. 'I wish I'd never started this now, for fuck's sake!'

Some time between the main course and the brandies,

Gal sneaked away from the table pretending to go to the Gents again. He had spotted a pay-phone at the foot of the flight of stairs near the toilets and he wanted to call Deedee before he was too drunk to make sense.

He dialled the number, but a loud electronic tone reminded him that he'd forgotten the international code.

Fucking hell.

A nervous-sounding Deedee picked up the phone on his third attempt. Hearing her voice and, more importantly, the fear in his own voice was a bad thing for Gal. It reminded him just how scared he was.

'You can still get out,' said Deedee. 'Fly out in the morning before they know you've gone. We can go anywhere. We don't have to be here, as long as I've got you . . .'

Deedee was having another one of her flight fantasies, in which running away was the answer to all their problems.

'Come on, love, come on,' Gal reassured her. 'This will be all right. This is the mighty Jabambo, remember? It's only one more day, darlin', just one more day. If you look at it like that, that's all it is, just one more day. I'm just playing it step by step – that's all I can do.'

On the other end, Deedee was close to tears.

'Deedee, I love you like a rose loves rainwater. Like a leopard loves his partner in the jungle. Like . . . I don't know what like . . .' said Gal, running out of comparisons. 'The point is, I love you! I really, really love you.'

Gal listened as Deedee told him the same thing.

'Yeah, I know that, you know. I know that, and I know you love me because I feel strong. I'd better go now – get back to the table before they start missing me. I'm gonna hang up now. Just do one thing for me, just one thing. Just say my name for me, just once . . .'

Far away in the darkness of their bedroom, Deedee held the phone close to her mouth and whispered, 'Gal …'

Gal put down the phone, put a grin back on his face and walked back upstairs to where the others were waiting. When Gal got back to the table, Don was once again the topic of discussion.

'Has he fucked things up? Are we gonna be put on hold at the last minute?' a slightly drunken Pete was demanding.

Malky shook his head. 'No, if he turns up, then all well and good. But if not, we'll have to accept we're a man short – it's too late to get a replacement now. I can do his job anyway.'

'This came at just the right time for me,' piped up Dermot. 'Talk about perfect timing, I was fucking ecstatic when I got the call.' He leaned towards the others to speak slightly more confidentially. 'I was in a right fucking hole, I was. I made ten grand last week. Next day I spunked the fucking lot, didn't I?'

'Horses?' asked a voice.

'No, fucking worse. I went to a fucking casino, didn't I? Might as well've burnt the money at home – at least it would have kept me warm. It was my own fucking fault. What a cunt! What a fucking loser! 'Course, I've gone back home with my arse hanging out of my trousers and there's no fucking milk in the fridge, is there?'

Dermot pulled a face to indicate the level of his agony.

'Well, has she gone apeshit or has she gone apeshit? What a fucking barney we had! Jesus. I says to her, "It's all right for you when things are sweet, ain't it? You don't complain when you're swanning up Bond Street, laden with fucking shopping bags up to your tits, do you?" Anyway, when this goes all right tomorrow, with what we'll get out

146

of it, she can just shut the fuck up, can't she?' he finished, happy beyond words with the idea.

'Anyone for another drink then?' asked Malky, finishing his second brandy.

'If you're having another brandy, I'll have another brandy,' pledged Gal.

He could do with a drink.

22. Breakfast at Teddy's

Gal sat alone at one of the few occupied tables in the Grosvenor Hotel's dining room, silently nursing his hangover. He'd had worse, but it had been a very long time since he'd woken up alone, without Deedee to fuss over him. Gal's secret hangover cure was ice-cold Coke and he'd already been through the three very small cans in his mini-bar. (And a bloody rip-off they were, too.)

He felt marginally better when he started moving, and once downstairs he had ordered the full English breakfast. The waiter had not bothered to hide his disdain when Gal had requested a bottle of HP Sauce as his meal arrived. One was found from the darkest recesses of the kitchen and brought to his table within minutes.

Gal poured himself a second cup of tea out of the shiny silver teapot and picked up a knife to butter more toast. Glancing out of the window into the cold, grey street, Gal saw Teddy Bass getting out of his car.

Fuck.

Teddy slammed the car door and disappeared into the hotel entrance. Gal took another mouthful of toast and munched it very slowly, staring towards the dining room doors.

He's looking for you.

Gal watched the doors.

He knows about Don.

A man walked through the doors. Not Teddy. A waiter.

He knows what happened to Don. He's gonna kill you.

Another waiter came through the door, pushing a trolley loaded with plates.

Then Teddy appeared, his eyes scanning the room until they settled on Gal.

'All right, Gal?'

Teddy sat down at the table opposite him.

'Tea?' offered Gal.

'This phone call he made from Heathrow – tell me what he said again ...' ordered Teddy, abruptly, staring deep into Gal's eyes.

Gal quickly swallowed his food.

'Who – Don? I've told you ...'

'Tell me again,' said Teddy.

'Well, just that he got back safely, really. That's what he said.'

Teddy shook his head. 'No, he didn't do that.'

Gal was ready to shit himself.

'How do you mean?' he said, dreading the possible reply.

'Well, I mean he didn't do that!'

Fuck.

'Yeah, he did!' said Gal.

Bluff it out. He doesn't know. He can't know.

'No, he didn't,' said Teddy patiently, as if he was correcting a slow child who couldn't help it.

Silence.

'Don didn't phone you from Heathrow.'

Gal had no choice.

'Well, I'm the one that got the call. If you know something different, then tell me! I don't know, Ted – I don't know what you're trying to get at here. Don comes to see me – offers me the job – I says, "Yes please." He goes. Next thing I know is he phones me from Heathrow, "See you soon." That's how he left it,' said Gal.

Please, please, please fuck off and stop asking questions.

'But he didn't phone you from Heathrow!' insisted Teddy, forcefully.

'All right, then he phoned me from Timbuktu, and said he was calling from Heathrow – but he still called me,' shrugged Gal.

Teddy stared at Gal, eyeing him as if he was a difficult crossword clue.

'I'm not lying, Ted. Why would I lie? I'm grateful for the job. I'm here doing the job, aren't I? But where Don has fucked off to, I just don't know.'

Teddy continued to stare for another few seconds then said, 'OK, all right.'

He got up. 'Good luck for tonight,' he added simply, then walked away.

Gal watched the front of the hotel where Teddy had got out of the car, but didn't see him emerge. After five minutes, Gal couldn't wait any more.

Jesus, you are so completely fucked.

By the time Gal got up to his room he was in an absolute panic.

From the second that Gal had seen Don's stomach exploding from the force of Deedee's bullet, he had known that he would have to do the job. Looking keen to do it was the only possible way not to have Teddy, Malky, and a fair percentage of London's criminal underworld hunting him down like a rabid dog. Not that people had any great love for a super-cunt like Don Logan. It was just that killing your house guest, especially one offering you work, was generally rather frowned upon. It wasn't really cricket, was it, old chap?

Bollocks, was it.

Gal hardly knew what he was doing as he grabbed his holdall from off the floor and threw it on to the bed. He unzipped it and began cramming clothes inside. He dashed to the bathroom and returned with his toilet bag, cramming that in too.

What to do?

Even as he stuffed his bag, Gal knew that he couldn't run. If he took flight now, they'd know. Wherever he and Deedee went, they'd track them down. They'd track them down and kill them both.

Gal stopped pacing and stared at the bag. Running away was a lovely thought. A lovely, big, wonderful, stupid, suicidal, sign-your-own-fucking-death-warrant, kill-my-wife-and-myself-now-please, thought.

Fuck. What to do?

Gal slumped down on the bed.

What to do?

All things considered, Aitch thought that it was rather a good job. He was standing on Gal's patio looking down at the newly repaired swimming pool. Still empty of water, of course, its bottom was now in pristine condition once more.

Two Spanish workmen stood on the opposite side of the patio setting up a hose to refill the pool. Sitting on the patio wall, watching them closely, was Enrique. He had a large dressing on his left temple hiding the wound Don had dealt him. By the time Enrique had eventually returned home to his mother and four-year-old sister that fateful night, he had come up with the perfect excuse. He had dived into Gal's swimming pool, forgetting that it was empty of water.

'Only you could dive into an empty pool!' berated his mother. 'Were you drunk?'

'*Sí,*' Enrique had smiled.

'*Stupido!*' she had concluded.

Enrique looked over at Mr Aitch, who had decided that he was well satisfied with the job and nodded to the workmen. Deedee and Jackie sat watching from inside the house, as water once more flowed back into the pool.

Now all they needed was Gal.

Night. The front of the Imperial Emblatt building sat serenely in the darkness. The tinted glass revolving doors were utterly still and the lobby waited in silence for Monday morning when once again it would echo with the sound of wankers talking bollocks.

Five months ago, Teddy Bass had emerged from the same revolving doors fresh from his afternoon visit to the Imperial Emblatt vault. As he had walked out he had smiled to himself. The smile had said, 'I'll be back.' Teddy's brain had spent most of the next month overheating itself into a white-hot mass as he tried to work out a way of getting back into that lovely, shiny, air-conditioned vault.

Teddy's mind had started by focusing on the building's black-glassed frontage. But for the answer to his problem he'd had to go deeper, much deeper.

Tonight, the front of the building lay protected under its invisible collection of computer-controlled laser beams. Inside, the impressive marble foyer (which had won several international awards for the tosser that designed it) was deserted. The corridors and the staircases leading off from the foyer like a maze of spiders' webs were lifeless.

The unmovable, unburnable, unopenable, massive steel door of the high security vault was tightly in place, exactly where it should have been. Beyond it, long banks of mirrored-steel safety deposit boxes nestled, each in its special numbered hole. Nobody knew that Box HS3671 contained nothing more valuable than a cigarette packet. And, after tonight, nobody would ever find out.

Behind Box HS3671 was the endless thickness of the underground bunker that surrounded the vault. Well, the almost endless bunker. If you were an empty packet of cigarettes sitting alone in Box HS3671, you might imagine that you could hear a faint whirring sound – a noise like the workings of a drill, getting nearer and louder as the evening grew later.

If you could voyage invisibly through the wall, you would find the blackness of nothing but underground brick-work and concrete. But the drilling would get louder and louder. If you could continue through the wall, invisible and undetected, you would come to a small metal drill bit cutting through the bricks.

You would also see that the drill bit was just the end of a large and powerful tool, and that the tool was being held by a man in a wet suit and flippers. And if you looked really closely you might just be able to see that the man struggling to keep the drill in place, continuing its work of boring through the bricks, was Gal Dove.

23. Twelve men in a bath

Deep inside the tunnel, Gal struggled to see through the clouds of dirt that now polluted the water. Every time he used the drill to dislodge another foot of concrete, he also unleashed dust which had turned the water around him into a murky haze.

Things hadn't been too bad when the team had started work in the underground swimming pool of the Turkish baths. Drilling away the tiles and the relatively soft plaster behind them had been a piece of cake. Then they had to bore downwards, tracing a path beyond the pool to the west. The tunnel they were hollowing was just wide enough for two men to stand side by side. Its narrowness restricted the flow of water and meant that the drilling debris clogged the immediate surroundings, hanging around the workers in thick, opaque clouds.

Behind Gal, two more men held enormous lights, intended for deep-sea diving. As Gal drilled, his co-worker, Dermot, pulled away bits of loose concrete with gloved hands to speed the process. In such seclusion, time was their only real enemy.

Back in the main pool area, Jimmy, Andy, Pete, Nicky,

Malky and Bruno sat around the poolside, all in wet suits. The men were at different stages of exhaustion, some recovering from two-hour shifts in the tunnel, others only one.

Teddy Bass and Stan watched the proceedings from a distance, while Mike, also in normal clothes, helped the divers with their equipment.

Stan went over to the edge of the pool and looked down into the now exceptionally grimy water. He was getting worried.

'Seems really slow, Mike. Are we falling behind?' he asked, concern etched on his face.

Mike shook his head. 'No, we're doing all right,' he said. 'Gal's just gone down for his third shift. This type of drilling's right up his street. He did the Frasier sewer job in '85, didn't he? That's why Don wanted him along on this, I guess.'

'Keep pushing them,' said Stan, quietly, so only Mike could hear.

'Malky? How you doing?' Mike called to Don's brother who was taking a breather on the opposite side of the pool.

'This is killing my fucking shoulder,' complained Malky, trying to loosen the aching joint as best he could in the tight-fitting wet suit.

'Jimmy! Andy! Two minutes and you're in!' ordered Mike.

Jimmy and Andy, who were waiting on the poolside, pushed themselves into the water and Mike handed them their oxygen tanks. They slipped the metal cylinders on to their shoulders and tested the mouthpieces once again.

Teddy Bass saw the next shift getting ready and came across to watch the changeover.

'Everything all right?' he asked, one eye on the clock as ever.

'Seems a bit slow,' commented Stan.

Mike overheard, taking umbrage. 'Stan, you're a fucking old woman! Haven't I just said? Have a bit of faith, for fuck's sake! Ted – we're all right ...'

In actual fact, Gal was far from all right.

Far down in the ever-lengthening tunnel, Gal was drilling like a maniac. Raymond, having changed places with Dermot, watched in awe at Gal attacking the concrete – as if he had a personal grudge against it.

I don't need this. I really don't fucking need this. This is entirely fucking Don's fault. Here I am, in a fucking tunnel, drilling through the earth, in water full of shit, and is it fucking OK? Is it fuck ...

Gal stopped drilling for a second while Raymond pulled more broken chunks of concrete away. Although the drill had stopped, Gal realized that his hands were still vibrating.

You should be having a San Miguel, my son. A nice cold bottle of San Miguel ... feet up, sitting in the sun with a nice piece of spicy sausage on the barbecue. Friends nearby, and your absolutely gorgeous wife Deedee sunning her sexy body next to you. That's what you should be doing, my son. That's all you want.

Gal raised the drill to carry on, but Raymond tapped him on the arm and gestured behind. Gal turned around, the water slowing his movements to the rate of an Apollo moonwalk. Jimmy and Andy were floating there, waiting to relieve them. In an awkward underwater manoeuvre, the men exchanged positions, the confines of their surroundings making the procedure more intimate than felt comfortable. This was no place for claustro-fucking-phobics.

Gal and Raymond made their exit up the tunnel, partly swimming and partly pulling themselves along the sides. Gal broke the surface of the water first and hauled himself to the edge. He found himself looking up into the face of Teddy Bass, who stepped back allowing Mike to help Gal out of the pool, where he subsided like a beached whale.

'All right?' asked Teddy, simply.

Spitting out his mouthpiece, Gal managed a little smile as he gratefully inhaled unrestricted air.

'Glad to be back on the job?' said Teddy.

He's testing you.

'Like I never been away,' gasped Gal.

'Up for some more work, then? After this?'

Bastard.

'Let's see if I have a heart attack on this one, shall we?' said Gal, not committing himself.

Gal tried to read Teddy's answering smile, but, if he was honest, he couldn't tell what it meant.

Teddy walked off without another word towards the changing rooms. His shoes tip-tapped across the floor tiles of the shower area towards a figure who was bound to a chair. The man in the chair was called Cliff and he was the nightwatchman for the Turkish baths. Teddy had already had several little chats with Cliff, but now it was time to get just a little more formal.

When the boys had arrived that evening, Cliff had let them in. Buying Cliff's co-operation had cost next to nothing and ensured that their plan wouldn't go wrong before it had even started. Tying Cliff to the chair and gently beating him around the face were merely for effect, for the benefit of the police.

'Maybe you're happy with two-hundred-and-twenty quid a week wearing a sappy polyester cunt uniform ... Maybe you're happy with that ...' Teddy had said to Cliff during one of their early meetings, about a month previously. 'Maybe you don't like the idea of living somewhere in the sun, surrounded by beautiful women, loaded. Whatever you want, when you want it. But you've just had five grand. That's yours to keep, whatever you decide. You can leave now and take that home ... Or you can stay for the big one. It's up to you. What d'you reckon?'

Cliff had reckoned that he'd very much like to opt for the cool quarter-million.

'Hello, Mr B,' he chirped as Teddy approached. 'How's it going?'

Teddy looked at him slyly, then touched his finger with his nose, suggesting, perhaps, that Cliff should mind his own bee's wax.

'Sorry, Mr B.' Cliff acknowledged his gaffe.

'I know that you know this,' said Teddy, 'but I feel that this is an appropriate moment to remind you of exactly how the land lies regarding your future survival.'

Cliff nodded cleanly.

'Earlier this evening you were surprised by a gang of armed and hooded men who broke into the baths. They knocked you out, and tied you up in here, from where you saw nothing and heard nothing, right?'

'Right.'

'If I'm happy with how things are, then in one year's time you'll wake up one morning and be two hundred and fifty thousand pounds richer, with a nice new account somewhere far away.' Teddy leaned a little closer. 'On the other hand, if you ever even catch a cold in the same room as a policeman, then you'll wake up one morning – dead. Got it?'

'Got it, Mr B.'

'And not just you. I'll also have your wife chopped into

tiny pieces as well,' said Teddy.

For the first time that evening Cliff looked genuinely worried. 'I'm not saying that's not a good threat, Mr B, but it won't work with me,' he said.

'Because you're such a hard nut?' smiled Teddy.

'No – I'm not married.'

'Have you got a mother?'

'My old mum lives in Glasgow.'

'OK, so we'll chop up your mother instead. All right now?' enquired Teddy.

Cliff nodded, satisfied that he'd been properly threatened by a professional.

By the time that Gal was ready to start his fifth shift under-water, every muscle in his body wanted to commit suicide. As the unofficial expert in underwater drilling, he'd done more shifts than anyone else. Gal didn't care, though. Keeping busy was better than having time to think.

'How's it going, Gal?' said Stan seriously. It was becoming his favourite question.

'Well, we're getting there, Stan, but it ain't getting any easier,' Gal told him. 'Tunnel's narrow, and that floor in there is getting really rough with bits of fallen concrete. It's so fucking awkward. What time is it?'

Mike checked his watch. 'Ten to two.'

Teddy's face appeared behind Stan. 'How long we looking at?' he asked.

'At least another three hours, Ted. Maybe four,' guessed Bruno.

'Nah, fuck that,' said Gal. 'Two, maybe two and a half!' he offered more optimistically.

I've got a fucking plane to catch, mate, I have.

'It would be good if it was two,' said Teddy.

'We're all on it,' nodded Mike. 'Y'all right there, Malky?'

Malky was slumped at the end of the pool eating a curled-up sandwich.

'No, I'm fucking not!' he called back.

Mike went over to him and balled his fist.

'Give it some, my son. Give it fucking some!' he tried to encourage. Malky weakly balled his own fist, limply mimicking Mike's more energetic motion.

Gal was soon back at work in the tunnel. He floated in the water, drilling out yet more lumps with great difficulty. Beside him, it was Malky's turn to scoop away the debris.

Half-way into his shift, the concrete that Gal was drilling through suddenly became much softer. Gal guessed that he was now through the bedrock between the buildings and at the edge of the vault itself.

You gotta be near to it now, my son.

As Gal blasted away more rock, he noticed that no dust clouds were forming to hinder his vision. Looking closer, he noticed the dust was being sucked into the concrete itself. The water was draining away through a crack somewhere, taking the dirt with it. They were that close.

Gal caught Malky's arm and pointed out the welcome signs that they were nearing their goal. Close behind, Raymond gave them the thumbs-up and signalled that he would spread the good news and tell the others to stand by.

Making his way up the tunnel towards the brighter light of the swimming pool, he broke the surface and ripped out his mouthpiece.

'We're that fucking close!' he announced with a grin.

Suddenly, Raymond realized that he was being pulled

backwards in the water.

'Fucking hell!'

He looked around, and the others followed his eyes to see a definite current of water being drawn down the tunnel and out of the pool.

Malky appeared at the entrance of the tunnel, struggling against the water flow. Raymond grabbed his hand and pulled him away.

'Gal's behind me,' gasped Malky.

'Right! Get him out! Jim, get back from the side! Everybody get back from the fucking water!' called Mike.

Gal emerged at the tunnel entrance, trying to fight his way back into the pool. The current was gaining speed and strength with each passing second.

'Get Gal out!' shouted Mike. 'Now!'

24. Playground of the gods

Malky submerged himself in the water and let it sweep him near enough to Gal to grab his flailing arm. Together they fought their way towards the side of the pool against the ebb of the escaping water. As Gal reached the poolside and grabbed hold, he saw that most of the others were standing well away from the edge.

'Get out of there! Get fucking out!' Mike was bellowing.

Malky somehow found the strength to drag himself up and over the side, then he turned back to help Gal. A few seconds later, the two of them fell exhausted but safe on to the stained tiles that edged the pool.

The contents of the underground swimming pool were in the process of draining into the large security vault of Imperial Emblatt. As the uninvited liquid flooded in and hit the electrics there was a huge flash – strong enough to be seen in the pool area – as the entire security system shorted-out and died. Of all the eventualities for which the designers of that state-of-the-art system had prepared, having twenty thousand gallons of water suddenly flooding the vault wasn't one of them.

'Jesus!'

Teddy Bass grinned proudly. He had guessed right. What a fucking plan!

As soon as the water level had stabilized, the team dived back underwater again. They moved along the tunnel, armed with large hessian sacks and powerful sub-aqua torches.

The vault itself was now completely flooded, the water contained by the airtight steel door. Gal was the first to push his way through the large hole in the wall and enter the submerged security vault. Jimmy, Pete and Raymond followed him.

The men looked at each other wide-eyed.

Teddy really has fucking got it right.

All around them was row upon row of gleaming safety deposit boxes, and they had until dawn to open as many as they could.

Then Malky appeared, squeezing through the hole in the wall like a maggot eating its way out of an apple. He tried to suppress his laughter as he looked at the task ahead, but the sheer fucking joy was too much and a blast of uncontrolled bubbles erupted from his mouthpiece.

Gal picked up his drill from where it had been carried by the water current when he had been forced to abandon work and escape. He turned its tough metal tip on one of the security boxes and had the lock prised off in a few seconds. The others followed his example.

Pulling open the box, Gal revealed a black and white photograph of a married couple, unconsciously dating the clothes from some time in the 1950s. Underneath was a collection of what looked like love letters, held together with an elastic band. As Gal picked them, he saw the ink begin to smudge off the pages, leaking away into the surrounding water.

With the letters were a pair of horn-rimmed spectacles, a pair of delicate white lace gloves – and under those were two hundred thousand pounds in used fifties. Now it was Gal's turn to emit bubbles of delight.

Around him, the others were hard at work. Already the floor of the vault was littered with an assortment of sunken treasure: Rolex watches, rolled-up canvases, chequebooks, bonds, wills, deeds and credit cards. Floating weightless in the murky torch-illuminated water were dollars, francs, yen, and good old British pounds sterling.

Gal's next box contained a briefcase full of tax returns in neat leather document wallets. He junked that straight away. The next offered more hope – antique bronze figurines. Raymond had found a box with six hand-guns in it, together (worryingly) with a signed first edition of *Mein Kampf*.

To his great delight, Malky found a stack of pornographic Polaroids, demonstrating – in unmistakable detail – just how much (and how often) a famous newsreader loved her pet Alsatian.

Plastic containers filled with white powder were also proving very common, as well as tiaras and false teeth (in about equal measure, although rarely together). One person had used his box to store six tins of Heinz chicken soup ('Great New Taste!'), but the next one that Gal hatched rewarded him with a Fabergé egg, which he brandished at Jimmy in triumph.

A yellowed photograph of Rudolf Valentino drifted in front of Gal's face. He brushed it aside in slow motion and watched as Jimmy eagerly prised the lid off an urn. A dark cloud of what looked like dust erupted out into the water and Jimmy realized with horror exactly what kind of urn it was. He snapped the lid back in place and paddled the floating ashes away from him as if they were a swarm of mosquitoes.

Someone found an old carriage clock, someone else a Purple Heart medal. Another box revealed baby-shoes and a set of sparkling jewels. The vault floor was a carpet of glinting booty: diamonds, emeralds, sapphires, amethysts, diamonds, and more diamonds.

Gal opened what felt like his millionth box and rifled through it. It was mostly official-looking papers, but as he cast them roughly away, a pair of exquisite ruby earrings fell out and gently floated to the floor. Gal watched their slow descent until they hit bottom, nestling in between the other valuables. He leant down, straining the seams of his wet suit, and retrieved them. Next to him, Raymond and Malky were shovelling plunder into the hessian sacks. Jimmy was in the far corner, grabbing at soggy notes drifting around in the water.

Gal turned away from them and carefully, secretly, slipped the earrings into a small pocket in the wet suit.

Deedee.

'That was better than finding fucking Atlantis!' announced Dermot, raising the glass of cold beer in his hand. 'That was fucking cum, that was!'

The lads had taken over a private bar for the official post-job jolly.

'Yeah,' agreed Raymond. 'I'm only going to rob flooded banks from now on. The dry land sort can just fucking fuck off.'

'Ain't that right, Jim?' called Malky from the bar.

'What's that?'

'Fucking ashes!'

'Yeah, frightened the life out of me. Poor cunt! Wonder who it was!' He took a slug of his drink and shuddered. 'Yerk – hope I never swallowed none.'

Gal sat at a small table on the periphery of the action, nursing a small whisky. His holdall, already packed, was by his feet under the table. He was waiting for his chance to escape.

Raymond spotted Gal's solitude and wandered over.

'I'll tell you what, mate, you're a fucking pleasure to work with,' he said, offering his hand.

Gal shook it warmly.

'Cheers, Ray. Must do it again some time,' said Gal, wondering for the umpteenth time why he always felt compelled to say the polite thing.

'Me? Nah, this one'll do it for me. I'm getting too old!' sighed Raymond. 'I'm gonna sleep for a week after this!'

A chorus of 'My Old Man's a Dustman' burst from the mouths of Jimmy, Pete and Malky, inspired by the hessian bags they'd all been lugging around earlier. Stan and Mike waited to join in on the harmonies, but they never got the chance. A round of applause greeted the arrival of Teddy Bass.

He smugly surveyed the room, lightly applauding back.

'Gentlemen,' he said, with a smile so wide it was positively rictus, 'you're all cunts!'

More applause, and someone put a whisky in Teddy's waiting hand.

Gal took the tiniest sip of his own drink.

Get out.

Get out now while you can. You've fucking done it.

Get out.

'You tired?' said Teddy to Gal, homing in on him like a hyena to a corpse.

'No, I'm all right, actually, thanks, Ted.'

Silence.

Jesus. He's still at it.

Teddy and Gal tried to break the uncomfortable silence at the same moment ...

'No, after you. Go ahead,' said Teddy.

'No, I was just going to say, congratulations!' said Gal, his face still a mask of doom. 'It went like a fucking dream, didn't it? Best-run job I've ever done!'

'Congratulations all round, I'd say. You did your end brilliant. Just as good as Don said you'd be,' offered Teddy, carefully watching Gal's eyes for a reaction.

'Yeah ...'

He didn't get one.

'What's the matter? You don't seem too happy?'

Oh fuck.

Gal tried to brighten up. Just for Teddy.

'Who me? No, I'm happy. I'm happy all right! Well happy!' Gal assured him.

'Then we're all happy.'

Teddy looked down at the holdall under the table.

'What – you shooting off?' he asked innocently.

'Me? Yeah, I got a plane to catch ...' said Gal weakly.

'Have you?' said Teddy looking him straight in the eye. 'Tell you what, I'll give you a lift.'

Shit.

'No, you're all right, Ted. Thanks and all that, but I can jump in a cab.'

Teddy wasn't having it. He was already standing up.

'What – you a visitor from foreign shores, get a cab to the airport? Don't be silly. Come on ...'

Gal sat quietly in the passenger seat of Teddy's Porsche as they drove through the pre-dawn, drizzly streets of London. The only sounds that cut through the awkward silence were the purr of the engine and the gentle swish of the windscreen wipers.

Gal couldn't stand the quiet any longer. 'It went like a fucking dream, didn't it? Best-run job I've ever done.'

'You said that already,' remarked Teddy, coldly.

'All the lads are well happy.'

'Good.'

Silence.

'Getting the nightwatchman on our side was genius, Ted. No worries about getting in or nothing. Got started straight away.'

'I'm glad you liked it.'

Teddy shifted gear, speeding through an amber light.

'Did you leave him tied up or what?'

'How do you mean?' said Teddy.

'When you went back in to see that geezer, just before we all left, yeah? Did you leave him tied up for the police to find, or untie him a bit – like he'd escaped?' wondered Gal.

'I didn't do either.'

'No?'

'No.'

Teddy looked over and smiled, taking his eyes off the road for far longer than was comfortable for Gal.

'I shot him in the head,' Teddy told him.

Gal found himself feeling a bit sick.

'You don't mind, do you, Gal?'

Gal shrugged casually. 'No, I ... I mean, if that's what you reckoned was ... you know, best and that ...'

Teddy enjoyed Gal's discomfort, stringing it out for a few

tortuous moments as they drove on in silence again.

'No, 'course I didn't. I never shot him – he was a good lad. He'll keep his mouth shut,' said Teddy, lightly, flashing his eyes at Gal.

'Shit! You fucker! You fucking had me going there!' exclaimed Gal, not hiding his genuine relief. 'Ted, you fucker! Jesus!'

Fucker.

Teddy watched Gal's happy face, again enjoying the sight. He waited a few more minutes then said simply, 'No, I did shoot him really. Well, he was just sitting there, wasn't he?'

At that moment, sitting in Teddy Bass's car, hurtling through the damp, deserted streets, Gal realized just how much he didn't want to die.

25. 'Where's Don?'

Just past Kensington, heading west, Teddy turned off the main road.

'I've just got to stop off for a minute. Is that all right?'

Like I have a choice?

'Yeah, of course it is ...' nodded Gal, helplessly.

Swerving into another Kensington back street, Teddy pulled his Porsche up outside a huge Georgian town house and switched off the engine. Gal sat silently beside him.

Eventually, Teddy turned and said, 'Come with me.'

Gal followed Teddy towards the expensive house and watched as he pressed the front doorbell. They waited in silence until a light came on in one of the upstairs rooms. Teddy pressed the bell again and a few moments later a voice spoke to them through the door.

'Who is it?'

'It's Teddy, Harry. Teddy Bass – remember?'

'What do you want?' asked Chairman Harry's confused voice. 'It's ten past five in the morning.'

Teddy smiled at Gal.

'I know, I'm sorry about that, but I need your help. Something's happened. There's been a bit of trouble,' he explained.

The door opened slowly to reveal Chairman Harry standing sleepy-eyed in his dressing gown and pyjamas.

'What is it?' he said in a worried voice.

Teddy breezed straight past Harry without waiting to be asked inside. 'Come on in, Gal,' he called over his shoulder, as if he owned the place, then disappeared into the house's dark interior. Gal followed limply behind, like a stray dog.

As Teddy strolled into the drawing room, Harry, half angry and half scared, quickly caught him up.

'What do you think you're doing?' he demanded.

Teddy fixed him with those Teddy Bass eyes.

'I need a drink for my friend here – could you fix him one?' he asked, gently.

Harry hesitated, weighing up the situation. He looked across at Gal, who smiled back in an embarrassed I'd-rather-not-be-here-at-all kind of way. Then Chairman Harry moved over to the ornately plush drinks cabinet and opened one of the glass doors.

'What are you having, Gal?' asked Teddy, still acting the host.

'Erm ... I'll have a whisky, please ... cheers.'

Chairman Harry opened a diamond-cut decanter and poured out a large whisky. He looked over at Teddy.

'No, I'm all right, thanks,' said Teddy.

Teddy raised his hand, which suddenly had a gun in it. Then he shot Chairman Harry straight in the face, blowing out his brains and spraying them all over the glass doors of the drinks cabinet behind.

Oh fuck.

In the words of a recently deceased bastard, Gal was rather perturbed by this development.

Teddy walked slowly across the room and stood next to

the perturbed Mr Dove, the gun still in his hand.

'Where's Don, Gal?'

Gal's mind was replaying Harry's body being lifted by the force of the gun blast, falling back, crashing into the drinks cabinet, then slumping to the floor with a sickening squelch.

'Where's Don, Gal?'

Teddy waited patiently.

'You see, he never left Spain – I know that. He never got on a plane. Or rather, he did, but then he got straight off again. There's no record at all of him being on any other flight.'

Gal waited in agony.

'So I can only assume that he's still in Spain,' continued Teddy.

In his mind, Gal was hopelessly picturing his beautiful wife, Deedee, sitting by their refilled and repaired swimming pool. Teddy's voice broke into Gal's imagining, breaking the vision into a million pieces.

'Where's Don, Gal?'

Gal looked up at his tormentor. There were tears of fear and exhaustion in his eyes.

Fucking kill me then.

'I'm not into this any more, Ted,' said Gal, so quietly it was almost a whisper.

Fucking kill me and get it over with.

Half an hour later, Teddy's Porsche pulled into the kerb at Heathrow. To his great surprise, Gal continued to find that he wasn't dead yet.

Teddy lit up a cigarette and took a drag before turning to Gal. 'How much did Don say you were on for this job? One per cent? Two?'

'He said it might change and that, but he reckoned

two ...' said Gal.

Teddy reached inside his coat, searching for his wallet.

'Well, I'm gonna give you a tenner. Is that all right?' said Teddy, flatly.

Gal stared down at his feet, anything to avoid those eyes.

Teddy opened his wallet and tutted. Then he pulled out a purple note. 'I've only got a twenty. You got change?'

Gal awkwardly manoeuvred in the car seat, trying to get at the money in his back pocket. The two men exchanged notes, then Gal got out and took his holdall from the boot. Without another word, Teddy sped off.

Gal put down his holdall and checked the time. There was a while before his flight. He put his hands in his jacket pockets, wondering what to do next – and felt a pin-prick in one finger. He pulled something out of his pocket and stared down at the two objects in his hand. A pair of priceless ruby earrings ...

The sun blazed in the sky like a ball of pure hate. Around it, a perfect deep blue firmament stretched away to the horizon in every direction. There were no clouds or birds to interrupt the view, nor any aeroplanes to break the glorious sun-baked silence. Only Aitch.

Sprawled out on a sunbed, Gal Dove was slowly but surely being roasted alive. The hot-water bottle of spare, baggy flesh around his waist was turning a brighter shade of lobster red with every passing hour.

You are fucking home, my son.

To Gal's right, Enrique was also lying out on a sunbed. He smiled, basking in his new-found life of luxury.

'That is a load of bollocks,' came Jackie's voice, trying to hide her laughter.

'No, I'm telling you. Barbers are a thing of the past,'

Aitch was informing her, casually.

'Cobblers! Utter cobblers!' repeated Jackie.

'Look, with this pill, they're saying that you take it and that's that,' continued Aitch, enjoying himself. 'Your hair don't grow. You don't go bald. You stay exactly the same. You have your hair cut once, in whatever style you want, and it stays like that for the rest of your natural life! It's completely revolutionary!'

'But what if you get fed up with the style, you berk?' asked Jackie.

'Well, that's where the antidote comes in, doesn't it, smart arse! The whole process is reversible – you just take a different pill! I'm not saying this is gonna happen in the next couple of years, but it'll happen. Hairdressers are shitting themselves!'

Jackie could contain her giggles no longer.

'Will you please shut up!' she begged. 'I'll wet myself in a moment.'

'They did this test with three monkeys, right? Gave them all a Beatles haircut. They've been living with that for the past two years now, and apparently they seem well happy with it!' finished Aitch.

Deedee had had enough. 'I can't listen to this,' she laughed.

Aitch looked over to Gal's sunbed.

'You all right there, Gal? You're a bit quiet, like,' he remarked.

'I am,' said Gal, 'fucking perfect.'

Gal looked over to where his beautiful wife, Deedee, was stretched out sunning her sexy body. Then he gazed down into his swimming pool, once more full of cool, clear water. He admired the new tiles at the bottom of the pool. The design still showed two hearts, but now they were entwined more closely than ever.

In his mind, Gal could hear the rasping monotone of Don Logan's voice.

'Told ya you'd do the job!' he was saying, sounding thoroughly pleased with himself.

Gal stared at the mosaic hearts, knowing they'd never be broken again. They'd better bloody well not be – he knew what was under them.

'Yeah, well, you were right, technically speaking,' Gal answered Don in his head. 'But you can shut up – you're dead.'

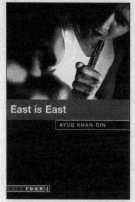

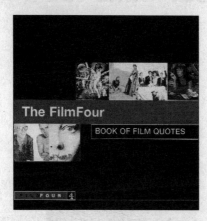

Essential Soundtracks
The New Movie Collection

Essential Soundtracks

40 tracks - the new movie collection

The Matrix • Fight Club • The Beach
Human Traffic • Austin Powers • The Sixth Sense
Eyes Wide Shut • The World Is Not Enough

FILMFOUR 4

Essential Soundtracks
The New Movie Collection

Includes hits from The Beach, The Matrix, Summer of Sam,
Buena Vista Social Club, East is East and many more

Double album available in all good record stores